PURRFECTLY DEAD

THE MYSTERIES OF MAX 20

NIC SAINT

PURRFECTLY DEAD

The Mysteries of Max 20

Copyright © 2020 by Nic Saint

Edited by Chereese Graves

www.nicsaint.com

Give feedback on the book at: info@nicsaint.com

facebook.com/nicsaintauthor
@nicsaintauthor

First Edition

Printed in the U.S.A

PROLOGUE

*P*amela Witherspoon was walking her Pomeranian like she did every night. She took her usual route past Hampton Cove park, and watched and listened to the rare spectacle of dozens of cats all gathering in the park's playground and yowling up a storm.

Why they did this was anyone's guess. People had wondered about the strange ritual for years, and even zoologists had studied the phenomenon and been left stumped.

No one knew exactly what drove all of these cats to gather in the same spot night after night and make these strange and frankly disturbing sounds.

Dirk Benedict, world-renowned zoologist and self-declared feline specialist, had suggested that it might have something to do with this particular spot. That perhaps located in the heart of the park was an ancient burial ground where the original inhabitants of Long Island had buried their cats, and now these modern-day cats, through some ancient wisdom, came together to honor the memory of their ancestors.

Others, like Laurence Tureaud, the famous ufologist,

1

thought this was probably the spot where aliens would one day land, when and if they finally decided on their invasion, and cats, being the mystical creatures they are, acted as the harbingers of this doom.

And then of course there were the more exotic of explanations. Some people, most notable amongst whom the renowned geologist Dwight Schultz, claimed the earth's crust was particularly thin in this exact spot, and the cats' yowls were a way of communicating with their counterparts living in the earth's core, which, still according to Mr. Schultz's more outlandish musings, wasn't solid iron and nickel, as most scientists agreed it was, but a large and complicated cave system where our counterparts live.

Pamela didn't care one hoot about all of those theories. She quite enjoyed the spectacle, and thought it was pretty. Boomer, though, didn't think it was pretty at all. On the contrary. The peppy little Pomeranian never stopped barking at the cats' meows, which from time to time earned him a shoe aimed in his direction. Usually these shoes were meant for the cats, but Boomer sometimes happened to be collateral damage.

"Pretty, isn't it, Boomer baby?" asked Pamela now.

"Woof, woof!" said Boomer in response.

"Don't you wish you were a cat in moments like these, Boomer?" asked Pamela. "So you could sing along with the rest of your lovely little friends?"

"Warrrrf!"

Pamela smiled. Oh, how she wished sometimes she could talk to her Boomer, and understand what he said. She was pretty sure he was the smartest doggie on the planet, and every bark that rolled from his lips a nugget of wisdom.

"My own precious little genius," she said now, as she took a plastic baggie from her pocket and crouched down to clean up Boomer's doo-doo.

There had been a rumor flying around about a new rule instigated by Chief Alec that dogs would have to use a litter box from now on, but so far she hadn't heard any more.

And as she walked on, Boomer straining at the leash to get at those darn cats howling up a storm, she suddenly came upon a strange and frightening sight: a man was staggering in her direction, his arms outstretched, his fingers grasping the air!

Boomer, who'd noticed the same thing, now redirected his attention from the offending cats to the offending stranger.

And as the man reached the circle of light cast by a street-lamp, Pamela saw to her horror that his face was white as a sheet, and his skin was devastated by dozens of open sores covering its acreage. In fact it wasn't too much to say that the man looked… dead!

She uttered an involuntary little yelp of fear as the man picked up his pace and moved in her direction, his clawing hands clearly yearning to grab hold of her!

"Come on, Boomer!" said Pamela as she turned on her heel and started walking away.

The man wasn't deterred. As she glanced over her shoulder, she saw to her dismay he'd picked up his pace and was now stumbling after her, a lumbering quality to his gait.

"Run, Boomer, run!" Pamela yelled, and as she followed her own advice, they were soon running at a rapid clip, trying to escape the horrid and menacing creature.

And she'd just turned a corner when she almost bumped into a large and voluminous figure. To her not inconsiderable relief it was Chief Alec himself, Hampton Cove's stalwart chief of police.

"Chief!" she cried. "Someone is chasing me!"

"Easy now, Pamela," said the Chief in his easygoing and reassuring way. He was a man with very little hair left on top of his scalp, and a considerable paunch, and was loved by all Hampton Covians for his kindly demeanor and years of consistent selfless service.

The cop was glancing beyond her now, at the corner where any moment the stalker would appear.

"I was walking my Boomer, minding my own business, when suddenly I saw this horrible, horrible creature. And he must have seen me, too, for he immediately gave chase. Oh, Chief. Am I glad to see you!"

She'd clasped a hand to her chest, which was heaving, her heart beating a mile a minute.

"You're all right now, Pamela," rumbled the Chief. "You're perfectly safe with me."

They were both still staring at the corner, but of her assailant there was no trace.

"I swear he was right behind me, Chief," said Pamela, starting to feel a little silly now. It's one thing to be chased by a monster, but another for that monster to suddenly get cold feet the moment the constabulary arrives. She secretly wished now her assailant would show his ugly face so the Chief could see for himself she wasn't making this up.

"Let's take a look," said the Chief now. She saw that his right hand was on his weapon, and as she stayed safely behind the man's broad back, she followed as he approached the corner of the park, then cautiously glanced around it.

"And?" she asked, her voice strained. "Is he still there?"

"Weirdest thing," grumbled the Chief.

She ventured from behind the safety of the police officer, and took a look for herself. To her surprise, the man was gone.

"Oh," she said, and even Boomer seemed surprised, for he suddenly stopped yapping.

She was growing a little hot under her collar when the Chief directed a curious look at her, the kind of look a doctor would award a patient just before calling the loony bin.

"He was there, Chief, I swear," she said.

"Oh, I believe you, Pamela. I do." But it was obvious from his demeanor that he didn't. "So can you describe this man to me?"

She nodded. "This is going to sound a little strange, Chief, but the man looked like…" She sank her teeth into her lower lip.

"Yes?" he prompted. "He looked like what?"

"Well, he looked like a—like a zombie."

*L*ook, I realize that I'm one of the lucky ones. My human treats me well, my food bowl is almost always filled to the rim—except when Vena the veterinarian convinces Odelia that I have to go on a diet—and I have friends in high places. I'm referring to Dooley, who had opted to lie on top of the couch's back for some reason. I guess he likes his heights.

But some days even I experience this strange pang of unhappiness. That nebulous feeling that something is lacking and you simply can't put your paw on it.

Today was one of those days. It wasn't that my bowl was empty—when it is, I make sure to wake up my human by kneading her arm and mewling into her ear until she wakes up and rectifies her mistake. It was that, what was in my bowl suddenly failed to grip.

And I blame it on that TV commercial we'd been watching for the third day in a row.

Lately my friends and I have developed the habit of watching television in the early morning, long before Odelia and Chase are up.

Odelia leaves the remote lying on the coffee table, and we'd discovered—or I should probably say Dooley has discovered, quite by accident by landing his tush on top of the remote one morning—that one click on the big red button on the remote switches on the television, and a couple of clicks will take us to one of many shopping networks, which feature, every morning between five and six, a lot of commercials for pet food.

One of those commercials had attracted our attention, and we were watching it again now, all four of us on the couch.

"The revolution in pet food continues," a very beautiful young woman dressed, for some reason, in a white lab coat, was saying, smiling a perfect toothpaste smile.

"Pet food revolution," Dooley muttered reverently, as if trying to memorize the line.

"Peppard Nutrition Revolution brings you the latest scientific research and the highest quality pet food on the market. And the best part? It's free! Sign your pet up for our free testing program and enjoy all the benefits of Peppard Pet Food free of charge."

"She said free three times," said Dooley happily. "Which must mean something."

"I guess it means the food is free," said Harriet. She was smacking her lips at the sight of a gourmet dinner being presented now on the screen. Even though the woman with the lab coat always spoke of pets and pet food, the animals on the screen were all cats.

"Lucky cats," said Brutus as he shook his head. "What do they have that we don't?"

"Access to a good manager who got them into this commercial?" I said.

"We should be in there," said Brutus. "We should be the ones tasting that godly food."

8

"We could always ask Odelia to sign us up," I said. "I'm sure if she does we'd be selected."

"And why is that, Max?" asked Dooley, speaking from his high perch.

"Because Odelia is a famous reporter," I said. "And I'm sure these Peppard Pet Food people would love an article about their products in the *Gazette*, something which she could give them in exchange for our participation in this revolutionary new program."

"And I'm sure it doesn't work like that," said Harriet. "You probably have to know someone to get into the program."

"Maybe Chase could get us in?" said Dooley, obviously as eager as the rest of us to taste some of this 'revolutionary new pet food with the greatest taste and the highest-possible nutritional value on the market.'

"Chase? How would Chase be able to get us in?" scoffed Brutus.

"Chase is a cop," said Dooley, "and cops arrest people when they don't do as he says."

"I don't think Chase will arrest the Peppard people if they don't admit us into the program, Dooley," I said.

"Who is Chase going to arrest?" asked Odelia as she walked into the living room, yawning and dressed in her Betty Boop jammies and Hello Kitty slippers.

She took a seat on the couch and stared at the TV, her eyes still a little bleary. She and Chase had gone out last night on a date, and it had gotten a little late.

"We need to get into this new program," said Harriet now. "They promise its nuggets will add at least sixty percent extra shine to my coat."

"And make me lose fifty percent of my flab," I added.

"And make me seventy-five percent more butch," said Brutus.

9

"And make me at least forty percent more intelligent," said Dooley.

Odelia laughed. "This food can do all that? What is it? A kind of miracle cure?"

"How did you know?" asked Dooley excitedly.

On the screen, the woman in the lab coat now held up a can of that miracle food and smiled into the camera, her eyes shining with excitement, almost as if she'd tasted the food herself and loved what it had done for her. "Our scientists have developed Miracle Cure specifically with your beloved fur babies in mind. You will find that it doesn't just meet all of their needs, but makes them more healthy, strong, smart and gorgeous. Peppard Pet Food. The pet food revolution. And that's a promise, not a pitch."

"See?" said Dooley, practically vibrating with excitement. "It's a promise, not a pitch."

But Odelia didn't look convinced. "Miracle Cure? Sounds a little fishy, if you ask me."

"What's going on here?" asked Chase who'd walked into the room, barefoot and clad in a T-shirt that proclaimed he was the 'World's Greatest Pet Dad.'

"They've been watching one of those shopping networks," said Odelia, "and now they want to try this new pet food called Miracle Cure. A brand called Peppard Pet Food."

Chase stared at the screen for all of two seconds before he grunted, "Snake oil. There should probably be a law against them."

"See!" said Dooley. "Chase is going to arrest them—this is our in, you guys!"

"It's actually not available in stores yet," I said. "The only way to get the food is by entering your pets into their free testing program. Which is free," I added, hoping to convey some of my enthusiasm. "Free as in, it doesn't cost any money."

Odelia raised an eyebrow. "Don't tell me. You want to be entered into this program?"

"Yes, please!" we all shouted simultaneously.

She shook her head. "Oh, come on. It's probably just a marketing push for some new and dodgy product."

A phone number had appeared on the screen, and I now nudged Odelia's phone, which she'd left on the couch the night before.

She laughed and picked it up. "Okay, okay! I get the message." She tapped the number into her phone as Chase walked into the kitchen, shaking his head. He might be the world's greatest pet dad, but Odelia clearly was the world's greatest cat lady.

Moments later, she was talking to the Peppard Pet Food people, or at least I assumed that she was. And when she hung up she said, "It was an answering service but I left my name and number and told them I have four fur babies who can't wait to get their paws on some of those Miracle Cure nuggets," we all shared a look of utter excitement.

"You know what this means, right?" said Harriet. "We're going to be Miracle Cure pets!"

"*If* you're selected," said Odelia, dampening our excitement. "And *if* I approve of the program."

So we all crossed our digits that we would be selected, and that Odelia would approve our entry into the program.

Frankly, after having sampled every available brand of cat kibble and soft food on the market, I was dying to try something new.

Like I said, I know I'm one of the lucky ones, but even the lucky ones get bored.

Dooley had jumped down from the couch and was now tripping toward the pet door.

"Hey, where are you going?" asked Harriet.

"I'm going to ask Gran to call the same number, and also

11

Marge," said Dooley. "It's probably like the lottery. The more tickets you buy, the bigger your chances of winning."

See what I mean? Dooley hadn't even eaten this revolutionary new cat food yet, and already it was boosting his IQ!

*T*hings were pretty slow at the doctor's office, so Vesta decided to run into the pharmacy and pick up her prescription. Even though she liked to proclaim she was as healthy as a woman half her age or less, she still was plagued with little aches and pains from time to time. Lucky for her then that her daughter had married a fine doctor, who, even though he sometimes liked to express his desire for her expedient expiration, still tried to make sure she lived as long and as happy a life as he could manage in his medical wisdom and expertise.

She walked into the pharmacy on Downing Street now and the first person she saw was Scarlett Canyon. The woman's puffy lips puffed some more, and her cat's eyes flashed even more catty than usual when she spotted her mortal enemy. She smiled.

"Oh, hi, Vesta, darling," she said in unctuous tones that reeked of insincerity. "So nice to see you."

"Scarlett," Vesta grunted unhappily. For a moment she debated turning around and walking out again, but Scarlet had seen her, and so had the half a dozen other customers waiting in line, so she forced herself to close the door behind her and proceed inside.

"So what's ailing you?" asked Scarlett. "Heart palpitations? Wonky bladder? Cancer?"

"None of the above," said Vesta, carefully hiding her prescription behind her back. "How about you? Hemorrhoids? Flatulence? Venereal disease?"

Scarlett laughed a raucous laugh. "Oh, Vesta. You're such a hoot!"

Blanche Captor, one of the women in front of them in line, turned and said in a low voice, "Did you hear what happened to Pamela Witherspoon last night?"

Immediately all eyes turned to her. There's nothing like small-town gossip to draw people closer together. Even Vesta and Scarlett momentarily forgot their feud as they turned their attention to Blanche, a woman with cleavage as deep as her desire to gossip.

"She accosted your son last night, Vesta."

"Alec? What do you mean?" asked Vesta. She knew that her son was a real catch, being a widower with a steady job and all, but she could hardly imagine Pamela Witherspoon throwing herself in his arms. Alec might be a catch, but even though his mother, she was keenly aware her son wasn't exactly a Brad Pitt or Chris Hemsworth..

"She said she was being attacked, but when Chief Alec went to look for her attacker, he was nowhere to be found!"

"An attacker!" said Ida Baumgartner excitedly. She was one of Tex's regulars.

Blanche nodded. "By the park. Late last night."

"I heard it was a rapist," said Marcie, who was Vesta's neighbor. "And the Chief barely managed to save her. Pamela's clothes were all torn and tattered, and by the time she fell into the Chief's arms, she was only half dressed."

"A half-naked Pamela Witherspoon in the arms of a

widower. Now really," said Scarlett, clucking her tongue with delight.

"Oh, baloney," said the pharmacist, a no-nonsense older gentleman answering to the improbable name of Rory Suds. "Pamela was in here first thing this morning, and she told me the whole story." All attention now focused on the pharmacist, who seemed to bask in it. "It wasn't just a man she saw. It was a zombie!"

"A zombie!" said Scarlett, clutching her not inconsiderable chest.

"Zombies don't exist, Rory," said Marcie. "Everybody knows that."

"Well, she swore up and down that that was what she saw: a real live zombie."

"That's a contradiction in terms," said Vesta. "Zombies, as a rule, are dead."

"It is possible," said Blanche, "that Pamela had been drinking. I walked past St. John's Church the other day and saw her coming out with Victor Ball." She gave her audience a meaningful look, and they all gasped in shock once more.

The whole town knew Victor Ball as a recovering alcoholic, and to be seen with him was as much as an admission of guilt—of having issues with the bottle oneself.

"Victor is sober now," said Vesta. "He told me so."

"But he's still going to Father Reilly's AA meetings," said Scarlett. "And so, apparently, is Pamela Witherspoon."

Lips were pressed together, and silent looks exchanged. It was determined therefore, and writ large in the town's lore, that Pamela Witherspoon was a raging alcoholic who had taken to accosting police chiefs in the middle of the night, half-naked and rambling on about non-existing zombies.

Rory Suds shook his grizzled head, quickly worked his way through the line of customers, and when it was finally

Scarlett's turn, she cleared her voice, and said, clear as a bell, "My usual prescription for the contraceptive pill, Rory."

Vesta's head jerked up, as if stung. "Now Scarlet, really," she said. "You're not still trying to convince me you're on the pill, are you?"

"I'm not trying to convince you of anything," said Scarlett with a little laugh. "I'm on the pill, that's a fact."

"But you're my age! You passed menopause two or three decades ago!"

"Speak for yourself," said Scarlett snippily. "You may have passed your menopause but I haven't. And that's because I've been taking care of myself. As you know, I'm very sexually active, and therefore I need to protect myself from unwanted pregnancies."

"Unwanted pregnancies! You couldn't get pregnant if the Holy Ghost came down and impregnated you himself!"

Rory had returned with Scarlett's prescription and now placed it on the counter. "That'll be nineteen ninety-nine," he said, rubbing his hands with glee. He was having a good sales morning. His smile vanished when Vesta grabbed the box and stared at it.

"Um, Vesta, you can't just grab someone else's medication," he pointed out.

"Yes, Vesta," said Scarlett with a smile. "That's just plain rude."

But Vesta was studying the pillbox closely. "This is impossible," she said. "Rory, you don't believe this nonsense, do you? A woman of seventy-five can't possibly still be on the pill, right?"

Rory tilted his head. "I'm afraid I'm not at liberty to discuss Mrs. Canyon's particular..."

"*Miss* Canyon," said Scarlett. "I never married, which is probably why I'm something of a medical anomaly. Isn't that what you told me just the other day, Rory, darling?"

Rory gave a curt and embarrassed little laugh. "It's really not my place to—"

"Yes or no, Rory," Vesta demanded. "Has she passed menopause or not?"

But the pharmacist merely tapped the prescription and shrugged. "Like I was trying to point out, it's not a pharmacist's place to make these kinds of judgments. If Scarlett's doctor prescribed her the contraceptive pill, he must have done so for a good reason."

Vesta now picked up the prescription. It was as she had surmised: written up by Tex. She frowned darkly. "I don't know what game you're playing, Scarlett, but I can promise you this: I'll get to the bottom of your so-called medical miracle and I'll do it right now!"

And as she stalked off, Rory called after her, "Vesta! Did you need something?"

But she was already slamming the door. Scarlett might have fooled Tex, but she wasn't fooling her. No way a seventy-five-year-old woman could still be in danger of getting pregnant. And she was going to prove it, too.

*C*hase Kingsley breezed into the police precinct and was greeted by Dolores, who waved him over the moment he walked through the door.

"Pssst!" said the grumpy-faced and heavily-made-up desk sergeant. She glanced around, as if expecting spies to pop out of the woodwork and listen in on their conversation.

"What is it this time?" asked Chase, who knew Dolores well enough to know she was eager to spill some gossip.

"It's the big boss!" she said.

"The Chief? What about him?"

"Listen to this. Do you know Pamela Witherspoon? No, well, good for you. She's a widow," she said, making it sound as if Pamela was some kind of monster. "And last night she jumped the Chief in the park! Buck naked, she was, and dragging him into the bushes, asking him to make sweet, sweet love to her right then and there, if you please!"

"Huh," said Chase. "And? Did he comply?"

"Of course he didn't comply, you idiot! He told her he was on duty, and as everyone knows, cops on duty can't just engage in any frivolous activity they damn well please. So he plucked her naked bosoms from his chest and told her to put some clothes on. And listen to this—he then escorted her home, like the sap—I mean gentleman that he is."

"Right," said Chase, too skeptical for Dolores's taste, though, for she frowned.

"You don't believe me? Ask the Chief. He'll tell you it's the God's honest truth. The only part of the story I'm still a bit fuzzy on is what happened after he walked her home. I heard she invited him in for a quickie, but my sources weren't clear on whether he was able to restrain himself and walk away, or if he went in and enjoyed some midnight nookie in the widow's lair. Ask him, will you?" she added, as she picked up the phone. "And then tell me." And as Chase walked away, she yelled after him, "Don't forget to ask him, Chase!"

He held up a hand and set foot for the coffee machine. He had no intention of asking the Chief anything, but had to admit his curiosity was piqued. No smoke without fire, was one of Dolores's favorite expressions, and he had to admit that more often than not there was some truth to it.

And as the Chief joined him and held out his cup for a refill, Chase eyed him with a keen expression on his face. "You look like you didn't sleep a wink last night, Chief."

"Oh, don't you start, too," the Chief grumbled. "You'll never believe what happened to me. Zombies!"

"Zombies? I thought it was widows that had kept you up all night."

The Chief rolled his eyes. "Dolores!"

"Yeah, if she's to be believed you've been up all night doing the horizontal mambo with Pamela Witherspoon."

"What?!"

Chase grinned. "You old dog, you."

"Listen," said the Chief, tapping Chase on the chest with a disconcerted finger. "I never touched the woman, all right? I was getting some fresh air when I bumped into her. She claimed she saw a zombie, but try as I might I was unable to locate said zombie, but I could tell she'd had a big scare, so I walked her and her dog Boomer home, and that's as far as it went. I never set foot inside her house, no matter what anyone says."

"They also claim she jumped you, buck naked, and dragged you into the bushes for some sweet nookie."

"Oh, God!" the Chief said. "Sometimes I hate this town, Chase. I really do."

"So zombies, huh?"

"That's what she said. A man with a face full of sores, white as a sheet, eyes wide and scary, dressed in dirty clothes. As she described him he'd just crawled out of the grave and was now walking the streets, looking for fresh victims to feed on. He chased her around the park until she bumped into me. At which point he mysteriously vanished."

"She hadn't been drinking by any chance?"

"No, as far as I could tell she was stone-cold sober. Besides, I know Pamela. She doesn't drink." He scratched his few remaining hairs. "It's baffling, Chase. Baffling."

"Well, I'm sure it was just a bum who scared the bejesus out of your Pamela."

"She's not my Pamela!" the Chief insisted, gritting his teeth.

"Whatever you say, Chief," said Chase, clapping the other man on the back.

"Please tell Dolores not to keep spreading these tall tales. I know she listens to you."

"I'll tell her. Not sure what good it'll do, but I'll tell her," he assured the older man.

And as the Chief returned to his office, shaking his head and muttering strange oaths under his breath, Chase took a sip from his coffee and promptly spat it out again.

4

———————

$\mathcal{T}$he moment Odelia and Chase had left for work, we decided to go on our morning rounds and collect some stories for our human. And if I say we, I mean Dooley and myself, as Harriet and Brutus had decided to go on a different mission today, namely convincing Marge to ask as many people as possible to phone the network and put our names up for that Peppard Pet Food Miracle Cure testing program.

Perhaps I should have mentioned that Odelia is a reporter, and a lot of the stories she writes are sourced by her faithful cats. You see, we like to roam around town and listen in on conversations of unsuspecting humans, then relay those stories to Odelia.

And as is our habit, we tracked our usual route: to the police station, where there's always stories to be found, then to the barbershop, which is also a particularly rich source, and of course past the General Store, where our friend Kingman keeps watch.

First things first, though: the police station. The thing is, even though Chief Alec is Odelia's uncle, and therefore genetically obliged to tell her everything that goes on in his town, he tends to keep stuff to himself, even though he probably should know better.

So when we jumped up onto the windowsill outside the Chief's office and put our ears to the window, I fully expected to discover some juicy little nuggets and tidbits.

I'd never expected the story to be quite as juicy as this, though.

"No, Madam Mayor, I'm telling you, it never happened!"

Seated in front of the Chief was Hampton Cove's new mayor Charlene Butterwick. She was blond and pretty, looking very professional with her snazzy glasses, and I would have put her around Marge's age. She certainly seemed more capable than the last mayor, who'd recently been arrested for a long list of crimes.

"And I'm telling you that it doesn't matter, Chief," said Mayor Butterwick. "It's all about perception. If people think you did something, in their minds you did it."

"But I never jumped the woman's bones, and she didn't jump mine!"

"The story I heard was that she was dancing naked under the light of the full moon, and that you couldn't control yourself and dragged her into the bushes where you had your way with her."

"It never happened!"

"And I'm telling you it doesn't matter if it did or didn't happen. This story is doing the rounds of Hampton Cove right now, whether you like it or not."

"Oh, dear God," said the Chief, rubbing his face. "I so don't need this."

"Do you think I need it? If we don't get this situation under control we face a big problem, Chief."

"Alec, please, Madam Mayor."

She smiled. "Only if you call me Charlene."

"So what do you suggest? A public statement? I could ask Pamela to come in and draw up some kind of formal—"

But Charlene was already shaking her head. "Won't work. People will simply say she was coerced into signing a bogus statement. No, we need to find this zombie and then we might have something to go on."

"Find what zombie?" asked the Chief miserably. "You know as well as I do that zombies don't exist."

"I know that, and you know that, but Pamela seems to believe otherwise, and so, I'm sure, will John Q. Public. If we can produce the zombie, and publish his statement, there's a chance this can be contained. Otherwise…"

"I'll talk to Pamela again."

"No! Whatever you do, don't go near that woman again. Not after what happened between you two."

"Nothing happened between us!"

"And that's why we need the zombie. He'll be able to confirm or deny."

"Do you think Uncle Alec saw a zombie last night, Max?" asked Dooley now.

"I doubt it," I said. "For one thing, zombies don't exist, and for another, clearly something else is going on here, Dooley."

"Uncle Alec did something to that Pamela woman, you think?"

"I don't know, Dooley, but he is a man, and he hasn't been with a woman for a long time, so…"

Dooley's eyes had gone wide. "We have to tell Odelia. This is a great story for her newspaper!"

"It is a great story," I admitted, "but not one Odelia will want to print. It's going to damage her uncle's reputation, and that's the last thing she'd ever do."

"But if it's true, she has to print it. It's in the reporter's code!"

"There is no reporter's code, Dooley," I said. "You're thinking about doctors."

"Don't reporters have an obligation to tell the truth, the whole truth and nothing but the truth?"

"Odelia does, but not all reporters are like her."

"So now I have to go out and find a non-existent zombie," said Uncle Alec.

"You'll do no such thing," said the Mayor. "Chase will find the zombie."

"And what am I supposed to do in the meantime? Twiddle my thumbs?"

"Until this matter is resolved, I suggest you go home, Alec. And that's not a friendly suggestion, that's an order."

"Go home! But..."

"I'm suspending you, and appointing Chase acting chief." She got up. "Go home, Alec, and in your own best interest better don't show your face around town for a while."

And then she was gone, leaving Chief Alec looking both stricken and dumbfounded, which is not an easy combination to pull off but he still managed it convincingly.

5

"We have to find this zombie, Dooley," I said. "He's the only one who can confirm or deny Uncle Alec's account of what happened last night."

"But didn't you say zombies don't exist?"

"No, they don't, so it must be a real person, and not a zombie, which is a good thing."

"How so?"

"Because otherwise we'd have to go to the graveyard to find the zombie, and I don't like graveyards."

We'd jumped down from the windowsill and were now passing by the barbershop, which usually is good for at least two or three stories a week.

We walked in, and settled ourselves near the window. Fido Siniawski, the hairdresser, was busy cutting a client's long mane. He was one of those so-called hard rockers, with the black leather jackets and the long hair, and had apparently decided to change genres and become a punk rocker instead, which meant he needed a Mohawk.

"Why is that man having his nice hair cut, Max?" asked Dooley as we watched on.

"Because he changed music genres," I explained. "He was a hard rocker, and hard rockers like to have the long greasy hair. But now he's a punk rocker and punk rockers like their hair to stand up and be painted in different colors."

"But why, Max?" he asked, mystified.

"I have no idea, Dooley," I admitted. "I guess it's one of those things that are a little hard for us cats to understand."

"Have you heard about the Chief?" asked the former hard rocker, now punk rocker.

"Yeah, terrible business," said Fido. "Who would have thought a nice man like the Chief would suddenly grope a woman in the bushes like that, huh?"

"Horrible," said the rocker, shaking his head and causing the hairdresser to almost snip off an ear. "Then again, I guess these authority figures are all the same. Can't keep their hands to themselves. The first opportunity they get, they jump some innocent woman and drag her into the bushes."

"I'll bet he's done it a million times, only we never heard about it until now."

"Yeah, I'll bet he paid off all of those other women, and Pamela Witherspoon is the first one who decided that enough was enough, and came forward with the story."

"She's a hero," Fido agreed as he studied the picture of a man with a Mohawk he was using as a reference. "And she should probably lawyer up. Get together with all of the Chief's other victims and sue the man's ass."

"I'll bet he's rich, though. He can probably afford the most expensive lawyers."

"Oh, he'll get off, all right," said the barber, snipping away to his heart's content. "All those rich bastards do. But I'll tell you one thing. This town will never forget."

"Never," the rocker agreed. He winced a little as the barber fired up his razor and went to work removing the last remnants of hair along a thin strip in the middle.

"This is bad, Max," said Dooley as we walked out of the barbershop and set paw for the General Store. "Uncle Alec is quickly turning into a persona non gratis."

"Persona non grata," I corrected him. "And you're right. It's looking pretty bad for him."

We'd arrived at the General Store, where Kingman, one of our best friends, likes to sit on top of the counter and help his human by keeping a close eye on the CCTV screens that cover the entire store. Whenever he sees something untoward happening, he loudly meows, and Wilbur has managed to catch a lot of would-be shoplifters in the act that way. Today, though, the sun was shining, and Kingman was sunning on the pavement.

"Oh, hey, you guys," he said the moment we hove into view. "So bad business about that uncle of Odelia's, huh? A serial rapist? Who would have thought?"

"Uncle Alec is not a rapist," I said. "Serial or otherwise. He merely tried to help a woman who claimed she saw a zombie and then town gossip did the rest."

"And I heard she was walking her dog and minding her own business when Chief Alec dragged her into some bushes, ripped off her clothes and forced himself upon her."

"None of that is true," I said, even though of course I hadn't actually been there.

Kingman gave me a hard look. "Well, I heard a cry last night," he said. "When we were at cat choir? That must have been Pamela, being dragged into the bushes by your Alec."

"It didn't happen, Kingman," I insisted.

"No, Uncle Alec says it didn't happen, so it didn't happen," Dooley confirmed.

"I don't know, you guys," said Kingman, holding up his paws. "But if I were you, I'd be careful around the dude. Obviously he's some kind of sick pervert."

"What's a pervert, Max?" asked Dooley.

"Um…"

"Your uncle Alec is a pervert," said Kingman. "And if he's capable of ambushing innocent widows, who knows what he'll do next."

"Look, Pamela Witherspoon saw a zombie, okay? And Alec merely tried to help her."

"A zombie!" said Kingman with a laugh. "A likely story!"

"No, but it's true. He was a man who looked like a zombie, and she was scared, so she turned to Uncle Alec, who just happened to—"

"—be lurking in the bushes with his pants around his ankles. Yeah, I know the drill. I've seen *Criminal Minds*. He's a pervert who deserves to rot in jail. And now if you'll excuse me, I have work to do." And with these words, he turned indoors and left us staring after him.

"Is it just my impression, Max, or was Kingman less than nice to us just now?"

"It's not just your impression, Dooley. I have a feeling cats are going to start taking sides, and if we stick with Uncle Alec we might just find ourselves left out in the cold."

"I'm not cold," said Dooley. "I'm nice and warm, in fact."

"Yeah, well. If this keeps up," I said, as I watched a cat I knew very well suddenly cross the street as we approached, "we might be moving to Alaska pretty soon…"

6

*V*esta Muffin had finally arrived at the office, but instead of greeting Tex's patients and telling them to be patient while they waited for their turn, she waltzed straight through the outer office, her domain, and into the inner office, the doctor's realm.

"Tex!" she demanded heatedly the moment she'd slammed the door behind her. "Is it true that Scarlett Canyon is still on the pill?"

On her son-in-law's examination table, Franklin Beaver was lying, while Tex was closely studying something on his hairy buttocks with a loupe.

"Vesta!" said the doctor. "You can't just come barging in here!"

"Hi, Vesta," said Franklin with a little wave. He ran the hardware store, and even in this awkward position still managed to retain a customer-friendly attitude.

"Franklin," she acknowledged. "So what's the problem this time?"

"Pain in my left buttock," said Franklin.

"You probably shouldn't have sat on that thumbtack yesterday then."

"Thumbtack?" asked Tex, dumbfounded.

"I didn't sit on no thumbtack," said Franklin, equally stunned.

"We all know you were drunk as a skunk last night and your so-called friends put a thumbtack on your chair at the Rusty Beaver as a wager to see if you would feel the sting. Clearly someone won that wager, as you didn't feel a thing, until this morning when you woke up with a distinct but sharp pain in your left cheek."

Tex, frowning, directed a closer look at the cheek indicated and then cried, "She's right! There's tiny puncture mark consistent with a well-placed thumbtack here!"

"The cheeky bastards," said Franklin good-naturedly. "I'll get them for this."

This mystery solved, Vesta returned to her point of contention. "Did you or didn't you prescribe Scarlett Canyon the birth control pill, Tex?"

"You know I can't divulge that kind of information, Vesta. Scarlett is a patient."

"Fine. I'll look it up myself then," she said, and stalked out again.

"Vesta!" Tex cried.

But she was already behind her computer, calling up the program that handled the medical files of their patients. She was momentarily stumped when a prompt popped up inviting her to introduce a password. So she typed 'MARGE' and the popup went away.

Tex, who'd appeared in the door, walked over. As he looked over her shoulder, he asked, "How did you get past my password?"

"Easily," she retorted, and typed in Scarlett's name. "And

when did you install a password? We're family, Tex. Family doesn't keep secrets from each other."

"These are medical records!"

"I know," she said, as she pulled up Scarlet's.

Tex held a hand in front of the screen. "I can't allow you to see this, Vesta. I'm sorry but I simply can't."

"Move your hand or you'll be sorry, Tex," she said warningly.

But instead of removing his hand, he pushed the button that powered down the screen.

"Oh, Tex. I wish you hadn't done that," she said with a sigh. And before he could respond, she'd sprinted past him and into his office, then closed and locked the door.

"Hey! Let me in!" he cried. "That's my office—let me in!"

But instead, she merely took a leisurely seat behind his desk and pulled up Scarlet's file, then calmly read through it, and nodded to herself. She then took a piece of paper, a pen, and jotted down a name and phone number.

"I knew it," she muttered to herself.

When she looked up, she saw that Franklin Beaver was still lying in the same position. She'd totally forgotten about him. He was smiling at her, so she held up her hand. "Not today, Franklin. But ask me again in a couple weeks." She waved the little piece of paper. "I might ask you to make a small… donation."

❦

*A*t the library, Marge Poole was reading a couple of chapters of Danielle Steel's latest bestseller. It had been quiet all morning, and since all of her work was done, she'd decided to skim the first page. Now, half an hour later, she was still reading, and hoping no new clients would walk in so she could keep on reading.

And she'd been so deeply engrossed in the story of a princess who marries a commoner only to discover his family are all members in good standing with the Sicilian Mafia, when suddenly the sound of a throat being cleared had her look up. Bertha Braithwaite had walked up to the desk so quietly she hadn't even noticed. The older woman was now staring at her with a distinctly malicious glint in her eyes.

"You have to renounce him, Marge," she said now.

"What?" Marge asked, her head still filled with scenes of mafia members suddenly showing up at the princess's wedding and threatening to shoot the place to smithereens.

"Your brother! You have to renounce him."

"My brother... what are you talking about?"

"The way he attacked that poor Pamela Witherspoon last night. I can't believe I never saw it before, but he has an evil streak. I should have known when I asked him to arrest my neighbor after he threw that dead mouse into my backyard and he flat-out refused. So here's my ultimatum to you, Marge Poole," Bertha said as she wagged a bony finger in the librarian's face. "Either you renounce your no-good pervert brother or you're losing my business, you hear? And not just mine. My friends are all saying the same thing."

"I don't get it, Bertha. What's going on?"

"Oh, don't you play dumb with me, Marge. Your brother attacked Pamela in the park last night. Forced himself on her and now he's trying to cover his tracks by acting as if nothing happened. But we all know what happened, and it won't be long now before his time of reckoning will come. I heard he's resigned already. And good riddance, too."

"My brother? Attacked Pamela? There must be some mistake," she said, stunned.

"No mistake. Alec has always been a dirty little deviant, and now everybody knows. So what's it going to be, Marge?

Are you going to tell him to leave town all nice and quiet like? Or are we going to have to kick him out, and you, too? Cause trust me, we will!"

"But Bertha!"

"Don't you but Bertha me, Marge. You have until tomorrow to tell your brother to pack up and leave Hampton Cove, or else we'll have your job."

And with these words, the old woman stalked off again, though this time without her usual stack of thrillers (all killer, no filler) neatly tucked into her big bulky purse.

Marge stared after this regular client of hers, stunned to the core. Then she picked up the phone and called her brother. He answered on the first ring.

"Alec! What did you do?!!!!"

$\mathcal{W}$e'd finally arrived at Odelia's office, a little later than usual, but with a big story to tell.

Odelia was typing away in her office, and when we walked in didn't even look up.

Only when we jumped on top of her desk did she finally pay us attention.

"Oh, hey, you guys. I thought you'd gotten lost somewhere."

"Uncle Alec just lost his job!" Dooley blurted out.

"Yeah, and he's being accused of attacking a woman in the bushes," I added.

Odelia blinked. "Wait, slow down—what?"

And in a few words we painted a picture of the things we'd learned that morning. Our human was staring at us, completely flabbergasted. The moment we were done, she picked up her phone and dialed her uncle's number.

"Straight to voicemail," she muttered, then thought for a moment. "What's the name of this woman? Pamela..."

"Witherspoon," I said.

"Dan!" she shouted. "Do you know a woman named

Pamela Witherspoon?!"

"We have her number on file!" Dan yelled back from his own office.

"Thanks!" Moments later, Odelia was on the phone with the illustrious widow, and then she was grabbing her purse and walking out. When we didn't move, she said, "Well, come on, you guys. Let's get cracking."

And so cracking we got.

"Dan! I'm going out!" she shouted.

"Great!" he shouted back.

"Strange way of communicating," said Dooley.

"Yeah, they do shout a lot," I agreed.

And then we were outside and jumping into Odelia's battered old Ford pickup. The vehicle might be old, but it still got us from point A to B. We hopped onto the backseat, Odelia put the aged thing in gear, and moments later we were creeping away from the curb, the engine making a whiny sound. The whine petered out after a while, as if realizing it could whine as much as it wanted, it wasn't getting to a mechanic anytime soon.

"I don't believe this for one second," Odelia was saying now, gripping the steering wheel in an iron grip. "Uncle Alec would never do such a thing. He's an honorable man. He would never attack a woman, much less drag her into the bushes and have his way with her."

"Well, it seems you're just about the only person in town who thinks that," I pointed out. "Most everyone seems to think he's guilty."

"Guilty of what, exactly?!" she cried.

"Let's hear what Mrs. Witherspoon has to say," I said.

We didn't have to wait long. Pamela Witherspoon lived close to the bus station, and after Odelia had parked across the street and we'd managed to cross without being turned into pancakes, she pressed her finger on the buzzer.

Moments later, the woman of the hour opened the door, looking harried. She glanced left, then right, then ushered us in. If she thought it strange that Odelia would have shown up with two cats in tow, she didn't show it. I think people in Hampton Cove are used to Odelia showing up with her cats in tow by now.

Pamela Witherspoon was a sixty-something plump woman with a jowly face. Her gray hair dangled in little ringlets around a high forehead, and as she sat down, a smallish dog immediately jumped onto her lap and stared at Dooley and me with a look of defiance in his eyes.

"Boomer, no," said Pamela as the Pomeranian produced a growling sound at the back of his throat. Obviously not big on cats.

"So what's all this about my uncle dragging you into the bushes last night? "asked Odelia, deciding to get straight to the point.

"Oh, I know," Pamela said. "And I swear it's just rumors. A lot of malicious gossip."

"Rumors? Are you sure?"

"Of course! Your uncle would never do such a thing. All he did was save me from that terrible zombie man and then walk me home so I would be safe. We said goodbye at the door and that was it. And then I went to the store this morning, and all I heard were stories about Chief Alec forcing himself on me. Crazy!"

"But where did those stories come from?" asked Odelia.

Pamela's face suddenly took on a note of embarrassment. "I may have had something to do with that. I told my cleaning lady this morning about what happened, and she must have misunderstood. And then she visited her next job and must have embellished the story, and from there the whole thing must have snowballed, taking on a life of its own."

"You have to stop this, Pamela," said Odelia sternly. "My uncle could get into some serious trouble over this."

The widow threw up her hands in a gesture of despair. "What do you want me to do? I tell people what happened but they simply won't believe me! Even my family and friends all think I'm lying to protect my attacker. They think I took your uncle's money and signed some kind of non-disclosure agreement and now I'm lying through my teeth!"

"Mh," said Odelia, thinking. "What if I interviewed you and put the story on tomorrow's front page? They'd have to believe you then, wouldn't they? Or we could even do a double interview, featuring both you and my uncle. Set the record straight."

"I don't know," said Pamela, shaking her head. "I'm not so big on interviews. And after the ordeal I went through last night I don't want my picture on the front page of the *Gazette*, Odelia. What if the zombie recognizes me and comes after me?" She shivered.

"What zombie? What are you talking about?"

"The zombie your uncle saved me from!"

Odelia plunked down on the couch next to Pamela. "Start from the beginning, Pamela, and tell me exactly what happened."

And so Pamela did. The story was a great one, full of twists and turns, and even the ending didn't disappoint: a vanishing zombie? That was the best part, I thought, even though Odelia clearly didn't think so.

"We have to find this person," she said.

"Oh, I know exactly where to find him," said Pamela, nodding.

"Hey, that's great," said Odelia, taking out her notebook. "You have his address?"

Pamela nodded primly. "The graveyard, of course. That's where all zombies live."

8

*A*lec was driving home, and stopped his car at a traffic light. He was still thinking about Mayor Butterwick's words—Charlene's words—when suddenly an altercation dragged his attention away from his own thoughts. For some mysterious reason people had gathered around his squad car and were yelling at him. Some were pounding the hood of the car, while others were trying their best to break the windows.

"Rapist! Murderer!" some woman screamed.

"I hope you rot in jail, Alec Lip!" a man was shouting.

"Let's drag him out of his car," a third person suggested, and tried to open the door.

Good thing that Alec always locked his doors, so as to avoid his car being the object of a carjacking. Still, he felt he probably shouldn't linger. So in spite of the fact that the light was still red, he stomped on the gas and the car hurtled across the intersection, one man still sprawled on the hood. Alec stopped suddenly and the man disappeared from view, then popped up again and screamed, "I'll get you for this, you rapist piece of scum!"

But Alec was already speeding onwards. He had no idea what was going on, and why this was happening to him. How could these people—*his* people—possibly think he could do such a horrible thing? Didn't they know him after thirty years on the job?

Apparently not, for as he cruised down Main Street, heads turned all along the sidewalk, and nasty glances were aimed in his direction, as well as insults hurled and even a Coke bottle that cracked his windshield. He shook his head as he sped up and vowed to heed Charlene's advice and stay home until this whole thing had blown over.

And blow over, it most definitely would. He was, after all, the town's beloved chief.

When he arrived home, he was dismayed to discover that all across his garage door the words, 'SHIEF ALEK IS A PURVURD' had been sprayed.

Oddly enough he was more annoyed by the horrible spelling than the actual message.

He clicked a button and the garage door trundled up, then he drove inside and the door rumbled down again behind him.

He closed his eyes and tried to relax. Finally home. Safe and sound.

His phone chimed and he picked up when he saw who it was.

"Hey, Marge," he said.

"Alec!" she practically screamed. "What did you do?!!!"

"Calm down, Marge. I didn't do nothing. It's all nasty gossip. None of it is true."

"People are telling me to renounce you or else they'll ask the council to have me replaced as librarian. And is it true that the Mayor asked you to step down?"

"She suspended me," he confirmed. "But only for my own safety and the reputation of the force. She'll conduct a full investigation into the allegations, which are all unfounded, and then I'll be back at my post in no time."

"I don't understand."

Frankly he didn't understand either. Only that morning he'd gotten up, a little grumpy as usual but still happy to go to work, and now he was suddenly rapist scum?

"You need to talk to Pamela Witherspoon," he said. "She'll confirm that what happened last night was all perfectly above board."

"Oh, Alec. Are you all right?" Sisterly affection came through her voice, and it warmed his heart.

"Yeah. Yeah, I'll be fine. I'm home now, and I'm not leaving here until this is over."

"You're coming round for dinner tonight, though, right?"

"I don't think I should show my face in town. And I'm not sure I should show my face at your place, either. If people see me, they'll come after you, too."

"Oh, nonsense. I'm not going to let my big brother fight this thing on his own. You're coming over and that's final."

After he disconnected, he smiled. The town might have turned its back on him, but at least his family was still in his corner. He now saw he'd missed a call from his niece, and put the phone to his ear.

Odelia picked up immediately. "Uncle Alec? I'm so glad you called. Are you all right?"

"I'm fine," he said, and then gave her a blow-by-blow of his eventful trip through Hampton Cove, and the way people had gone completely mad.

"We'll set the record straight," she promised. "I'm at Pamela's now, and she just told me the truth. I would like to interview you both and put the interview on tomorrow's front page, but she doesn't want to. She's afraid the publicity will make the zombie come after her."

"The zombie," he muttered as he rolled his eyes. He'd

gotten out of his pickup and was now walking into his living room, then dropped down on his couch. "Look, the best way to deal with this whole mess is to find this so-called zombie. He'll be able to confirm what happened last night."

"I know, but where do we find him? Pamela's suggestion was to go to the graveyard and locate him there. But that seems a little... impractical."

He could hear she was still in the same room with Pamela, or else she would have used a lot stronger language. He grimaced. "Maybe return to the park tonight around the same time? If this is a guy attacking women he might show up again, looking for his next victim."

"Good idea. I'll arrange it with Chase. I can play the victim and Chase can hide in the bushes, waiting for the creep to attack me."

"I'm not sure that's such a good idea, honey," he said, the thought of his niece being bait for some weirdo frankly appalling.

"Do you have a better idea?"

"No, frankly I don't," he admitted.

"I'll run it by Chase. Oh, and is it true that he's now the acting chief?"

"Yeah, he is. Charlene—Mayor Butterwick—didn't think it was a good idea for me to stay on as chief while she got to the bottom of this mess."

"Bad advice," said Odelia curtly. "Now it looks as if you're admitting guilt, and the Mayor is punishing you. So I'll talk to her as well. Don't you worry, Uncle Alec. I'll fix this."

And with these hopeful words, she rang off.

And as he settled back, suddenly a stone came sailing through his living room window, shattering it into a million pieces. He was on his feet in seconds, and when he looked out, he could see two neighborhood kids running away.

He picked up the stone. Around it, a piece of paper had been wrapped.

He unfolded it and read, "YOUR A DED MAN SHIEF RAPIST!"

He tsk-tsked. Again with the terrible spelling.

9

*O*delia had dropped us off at the house before returning to the office. When we walked in, I saw that Harriet and Brutus had made themselves comfortable on the couch, and were now intently watching that same home shopping network, with the Peppard Pet Food company's lab coat girl offering them the enticing prospect of snacking on Miracle Cure kibble for the rest of their lives.

"And?" I asked as I joined them. "How did it go?"

"Marge called the Peppard Pet Food people, and Gran called them, and even Tex called them, but so far nothing," said Brutus sadly.

"Maybe we should get more people to call in," said Harriet now. "I'll bet a lot of Marge's nice library customers would do her this big favor, and also Tex's patients."

"I don't think that's such a good idea," I said. "Marge is about to get kicked out of the library by those same nice customers."

"What? Why?"

"It's a long story," said Dooley, "and a very sad one, too."

"Maybe you can tell it, Dooley," I suggested. "You were there from the beginning."

Dooley's face took on an appropriately serious expression now that he'd been tasked with this very important assignment. "So Uncle Alec met a woman in the park last night and the woman saw a zombie and then people said he attacked this woman but it was actually the zombie who attacked her and so things got a little mixed up and now Chief Alec isn't Chief Alec anymore but Chase is and the woman doesn't want to have her picture on the front page of the newspaper because she thinks it will make the zombie come after her but if she doesn't Uncle Alec will never get his job back and maybe we'll all have to move to Alaska soon and be cold and live in the snow." He took a deep breath.

"Well done, Dooley," I said. "You gave a very good summary of the recent events as they transpired."

But Harriet and Brutus didn't agree with this assessment. On the contrary, they looked thoroughly mystified. "Alaska?" asked Brutus, as this seemed to be the point that had struck him most vividly. "We're all moving to Alaska? But it's cold up there!"

"I'm not going," said Harriet, shaking her head decidedly. "No way. Even though people always think I love snow, because of my gorgeous snowy white fur, I don't like snow at all. Not really. Snow is cold and wet, and I hate cold and wet. I really do."

"Alaska isn't the issue here," I said. "The issue is that Uncle Alec has been falsely accused and now Odelia is trying to clear his name."

"I think I could get used to Alaska," said Brutus. "I think all that snow and ice is good for your blood circulation. And of course you don't have to spend time outside. I bet inside it's always nice and warm. And cozy. You like cozy, don't you, sugar plum?"

"Oh, I do love cozy, sweetums," said Harriet. "It's the cold and the wet I don't like."

"Didn't you hear what I just said?" I asked. "Uncle Alec is being falsely accused of attacking a woman in the park last night."

"Yes, and now we have to find a zombie," said Dooley, "but weirdly enough Odelia isn't looking for the zombie in the graveyard, as you would expect, but in the park tonight."

"Zombie?" asked Harriet, finally dragging her mind away from Alaska and its no-doubt myriad pros and cons. "What are you talking about, Dooley? What zombie?"

"Well, Pamela Witherspoon saw a zombie, and then she ran into Uncle Alec, who saved her from being eaten alive, and now everybody thinks he dragged her into the bushes and did bad things to her, and if we can find the zombie he'll be able to confirm that Uncle Alec did no such thing."

"Clear now?" I asked, patting my friend on the back for a job well done.

"Clear as mud," said Brutus, but his attention was already wandering back to the screen, where the Peppard Pet Food company was doing a fine job of making all of our mouths water.

I shook my head and decided to take a nap. I had a feeling Odelia was going to ask us to tag along tonight on her zombie hunt, and I wanted to be fresh and alert. Zombies are not to be trifled with, and you never know when they'll attack and try to eat your brains.

And I'd just dozed off when I became aware of a strange sound. When I opened my eyes I saw that a cameraman was filming me!

I practically jumped from the couch, and as I stared into the lens, suddenly Gran's voice spoke in my immediate rear.

"That's Max, and the small gray one is mine. His name is Dooley. The white Persian is Marge's, and the black one is

45

Chase's, though he gifted him to Odelia, my granddaughter."

I looked up, wondering who she was talking to, and saw that a woman stood holding a microphone under Gran's nose. A fourth person was also present. He was dressed in a black silk shirt, red leather tie, and had wild electric hair sprouting from his head.

Next to me, my friends, also roused from their slumber, stared at the spectacle with as much wonder and surprise as me.

"Your family is really into cats, aren't they, Mrs. Muffin?"

"Vesta, please," said Gran, displaying an uncharacteristic full-toothed smile. "And yes, we all love cats. My daughter Marge and Odelia most of all. The men in our family, well, let's just say they tolerate our peculiar predilection." She laughed at her own joke, and the woman with the microphone laughed right along. She was very thin and young, with an abundance of dark curly hair and large-framed glasses. The cameraman, meanwhile, who was filming Gran, was a short and stubby individual with a round face and strange little beard that looked like a ring around his lips. He was munching on something.

"Thank you so much for inviting us into your home, Vesta," said Microphone Lady.

"Oh, no, I'm happy to oblige," said Gran. "It is, after all, something very special we're doing here, and the world should be our witness."

We all stared at one another, wondering what was going on.

The wild-haired man in the black shirt and red tie was pulling his nose now, and staring intently into the middle distance. "Are you sure there will be room for us?" he asked. "It's a very small place you got here, Vesta."

"Odelia has a spare bedroom upstairs," said Vesta. "And we have another spare bedroom next door."

"We could always stay at a hotel," suggested Microphone Lady. "I'd be happy to."

"No, we should be right here," said the wild-haired one. "We need to follow Vesta day and night. So I suggest I stay next door, while you two share the upstairs bedroom."

"Great idea," said Vesta, though the cameraman and the microphone woman didn't look convinced.

"Are you sure your family are on board with this?" asked Microphone Lady.

"Oh, absolutely," said Vesta, displaying another toothy grin. "They'll be thrilled."

arge was thoroughly worried. It wasn't just that Alec was in trouble, it was more that all of a sudden her entire world had been thrown out of whack. Alec wasn't just her big brother, the one she could always turn to. He was also the town's chief of police—the man *everyone* turned to. And now all of a sudden he'd been turned into an outcast.

It was almost as if she'd suddenly fallen down into the upside-down version of her normal world. As if she were living her own worst nightmare.

When she arrived home that night, after fending off dozens of questions from her customers, some worried, others irate, like Bertha Braithwaite, she was happy to be home. Happy finally to find a respite from a world that had obviously gone mad.

So when she walked in the door and was greeted by a film crew and a man who looked like Doc Brown from *Back to the Future*, it was frankly a little too much. And when her mother turned to her with a big smile and blithely announced, "I've decided to have another baby," she dropped to the floor and promptly passed out.

Lucky for her there were not one but two doctors in the house: her husband Tex, but also, quite surprisingly, Doc Brown, whose name wasn't Doc Brown at all but Clam.

So when she was quickly and efficiently revived, and found herself lying on the couch in a darkened room while muffled voices discussed her 'episode,' she thought she must still be dreaming, and for the briefest of moments thought that maybe the whole thing was a dream: the fact that her brother was suddenly being accused of a heinous act, and the fact that her mother had invited what looked like a television crew into their home.

But when Tex walked in and sat down next to her, a cup of tea in his hand, which he handed her, and a grave expression on his face, she knew it hadn't been a dream at all, but stark reality.

"Did I just pass out?" she asked.

"Yes, you did, darling. But nothing to worry about. Doctor Clam caught you the moment your knees buckled, so you didn't even hit your head or anything."

"Doctor…"

"Clam. Zebediah Clam." Tex's right eye twitched, something she'd never seen before.

"So who is Doctor Clam, and why is there a television crew in my house?"

"Um… maybe you better take a good long sip of tea first," said Tex as he tried to reassure her with a smile that came off more like a grimace.

But she took the sip, and then waited as he first cleared his throat, then inserted a finger between collar and neck and tugged.

"The thing is, darling, that your mother has decided…" He grimaced again. "Well, she has decided to…"

"To have another baby? But honey, how is that even possible? She's too old to have a baby."

"Exactly what I told her!" said Tex, slapping his knee. "But Doc Clam, who apparently is a fertility expert, claims it can be done. He claims that with the right hormonal mix the effects of menopause can be reversed, and even a woman of your mother's age can get pregnant and carry a baby to full term."

Marge stared at her husband, then took another sip of tea, hoping it would clear her mind of the sneaking suspicion not only Hampton Cove had gone mad, but her own family, too. "This is a joke, right? You're not serious, are you?" she finally asked.

"I'm afraid I am—and so is Vesta. She already started the treatment, and Doc Clam will be right here so he can take her case well in hand."

"And the television crew?"

"They're with Clam. He considers Vesta's case his most ambitious project to date, and wants to document every moment of her historic journey from conception to delivery."

"I don't believe this," said Marge, closing her eyes. "Tell me this is all a bad dream, Tex. Tell me this isn't happening."

"Oh, it's happening, and we're going to be in this documentary, too. Because Doctor Clam is staying in our spare bedroom, and his television crew is staying in Odelia's. Vesta was so kind to invite them to stay here, as the doctor feels it's important he's on the premises to monitor her progress closely, day and night. For nine. Long. Months."

"Nine months. Day and night," Marge echoed morosely.

"I'm… not entirely sanguine that this Clam's methods are entirely… scientific. Or even ethical. But when I tried to voice some of my objections, your mother overruled me. She said it's her body and her decision, and I should butt out. So I guess I'm butting out."

"I so rue the day I invited her to stay with us. I felt sorry for her, you know, after the divorce, and I thought I did the right thing by letting her stay with us until she got back on her feet."

"Oh, she's back on her feet all right."

She most definitely was. But then Marge took a deep breath and decided that this would pass, too. Her mother had pulled some crazy stunts before, and somehow they'd survived them all. And this time would be no different. She hoped.

"Say, what's all this I'm hearing about Alec attacking Pamela Witherspoon in the park last night?" asked Tex now.

"Oh, I completely forgot to tell you about that. Alec is the victim of a vicious gossip campaign, which has already led to his suspension as chief of police, and which might lead to my suspension as librarian as well. But Odelia is on the case, and tonight she and Chase are going to the park to look for that zombie. He's the key to this whole thing."

Tex stared at her, then wordlessly took the cup from her fingers and drained it.

Yup. It was one of those days.

Just then, the doorbell rang, and she got up to open the door. When she did, she found a stranger standing on the mat, smiling at her. He had a long white Santa Claus beard, long white Santa Claus hair, and was dressed in a red Santa suit.

"It's too early for Christmas," she said automatically, and made to close the door.

But then Santa pulled down his beard and said, "Marge, it's me—Alec!"

Uh-huh. Definitely one of those days.

11

*A*ll of our humans were seated around the dinner table, only this time three more humans had been added to the mix: Doctor Zebediah Clam, Libby Elk, who was a freelance reporter and documentary maker, and Jonah Zappa, her associate and cameraman.

Instead of joining the others for creamy prawn pasta, though, Libby and Jonah were filming, as if this were the scene of some reality show or *Lifetime* production. It was all very weird, and I wasn't entirely sure my humans were fully on board with the scheme.

Gran obviously was, as she was the life and soul of the party, giggling and laughing and telling anecdote after anecdote. In fact I don't think I'd ever seen her this lively and animated since making her acquaintance all those many years ago.

"Gran seems to be having a great time," said Dooley, making the same observation.

"Is it true she's having another baby?" asked Harriet, who looked slightly worried at the prospect.

"It sure looks that way," I said. "This Doctor Zebediah

Clam is one of the world's leading fertility experts, and he claims he can make it happen."

"But… isn't Gran too old to have a baby?" asked Dooley, putting his paw on the nub.

"According to Doctor Clam she isn't."

"I wonder what Marge and Alec will say," said Brutus. "About the fact that in only nine months' time they're getting a little brother or sister."

Judging from the looks on their faces, they weren't exactly over the moon, I thought. Alec, who'd downed both Santa beard and hair, clearly wasn't in the mood to become a big brother to a little munchkin again. His life was a shambles, and he clearly was harboring dark thoughts toward his dear old mommy. In front of the camera crew and Doctor Clam, though, the Pooles were all on their best behavior, and didn't offer a word of criticism, all keenly aware they were being filmed, their responses and reactions saved for posterity.

"I think it's going to be a happy occasion," said Dooley now. "Having a baby is always a good thing. A time for joy and happiness. Moments of love and light and laughter."

"I thought you didn't like babies, Dooley?" asked Harriet. "I thought you said they'd take your place and you didn't want them in the house?"

"I know that's what I used to think, but since then I've changed my mind," said Dooley. "And now I know that cats and babies can live together in perfect harmony."

"Very good, Dooley," I said, "And you're absolutely right. Having a baby is a source of great joy for any family. Soon the sound of a baby crying will be heard, and then the sound of its feet going pitter-patter on the kitchen floor. A great time for all of us."

"Tell that to our humans," said Harriet. "They look like they're at a funeral."

She was right. They did all look as if this upcoming birth was a funeral and not the happy occasion it was supposed to be.

Then again, even after spending all this time around humans, the species still remains a mystery to me.

"So what's going to happen next, Doctor Clam?" asked Chase as he sliced into a tomato and managed to spray some tomato juice all over his nice clean shirt.

The doctor steepled his fingers and looked appropriately serious. "Well, first I've started Vesta on hormone therapy—my own very special concoction. And then when she's ready we're going to perform the in vitro fertilization of one of her egg cells."

"Wait, what?" said Gran. "I didn't sign up for no frickin IVF! I thought this was going to go the natural way. You know, with me and some deserving male doing the deed."

"Please, Ma, don't go there," said Alec, holding up his hand. "I don't need that image in my head."

"I know what images you have in that head of yours, Alec," said Gran. "From what I heard all you can think about is you and Pamela Witherspoon getting jiggy in the bushes."

"Ma!" said Marge. "How can you even think such a thing?"

"What? Alec getting jiggy with Pamela? It's only natural. A half-naked woman jumps into his arms? Any man would be tempted, and especially a widower like Alec."

"Is that the story you heard?" asked Odelia.

"Sure. At the pharmacy this morning. Blanche Captor and Ida Baumgartner were talking up a storm. How a half-naked or fully-naked Pamela—depending on who told the story—jumped Alec's bones and they got hot and heavy in the bushes. And I'm happy for you, Alec. I'm happy you finally found yourself a girlfriend. Even though you probably should be careful, because according to all accounts Pamela

Witherspoon is a lush who sees zombies everywhere she goes."

"Looks like the story has changed a little since this morning," said Odelia.

"Yeah, the latest version is that Alec attacked an innocent Pamela as she was walking along the road, dragged her into the bushes and went all caveman on her," said Marge.

"I think I like Ma's version better," said Alec now.

"Wait, can you give us a little more background?" asked Libby Elk, the reporter.

"Well, my brother Alec, who is our chief of police," Marge said, "has been falsely accused of doing something very bad to Pamela Witherspoon. Isn't that right, honey?"

Odelia nodded. "The gossip mill running amok. It happens."

"Look, who cares about Pamela Witherspoon?" said Vesta. "I already selected a father for my future child and now you're telling me I can't even go the full monty with the guy?"

"The chances of you getting pregnant the natural way are practically nil," said Doctor Clam. "So I'm afraid in vitro is the only way we will be able to pull this off, Vesta."

"Well, holy moly. I'm having a test tube baby *and* will be the oldest mother in history? *Guinness Book of Records* here I come!"

"Are you sure this is such a good idea?" asked Marge, always the voice of reason in our family.

"Sure? Of course I'm sure! Look, when I had you two I was full of hopes and dreams. I thought Marge would become the first female president of this country, and Alec could blaze the trail for her by becoming president first, and now look at you: a librarian and a cop! What a disappointment! So now that I'm getting a second chance to get it right

"Nice," said Marge.

"Yeah, real nice, Ma," said Alec.

"You're welcome," she said, and popped a prawn into her mouth.

"So who's the father going to be?" asked Chase.

"Oh, I have someone in mind you're all gonna love."

"Who?" asked Marge.

She smiled. "Let's just say it'll be a nice surprise."

12

That evening, Odelia officially invited us to go zombie-hunting. I know I should have been excited, as I'd never engaged in such an activity before, but frankly I was a little trepidatious. Personally I don't know any zombies, but from what I've heard they're not very nice creatures and can, when provoked, turn vicious and downright nasty.

So it was with a heart weighed down with the weight of woe that I set paw in Odelia's pickup and allowed myself to be transported to the town park, where the nocturnal vigil was taking place.

Odelia, dressed for the occasion in a tank top, short-short skirt and a blond wig, looked as if she wasn't there to pick up zombies but men. In other words, she looked like Julia Roberts in *Pretty Woman*.

"Are you sure this is going to work?" she asked nervously as she pulled down her skirt, which was showing so much leg it almost appeared as if she was nothing but legs. She was also on high heels and in fishnet stockings. The end result was supposed to look sexy, but I guess I'm not the right audience, as I didn't think it was all that sexy-looking at all.

"I think it's going to work wonders," said Chase, the only one who seemed confident in the scheme. "If that zombie sees you, he's going to try to jump you so fast it'll make your head spin."

"My head is spinning already," she said, "but that may have something to do with this wig. It's really tight around my head."

"Has to be, babe, or it will fall off."

"So what are we supposed to do?" I asked, and I think I was speaking for the entire cat contingent when I posed this question.

"You just keep a close eye on the proceedings," she said. "And if you see any sign of the zombie, you holler."

Well, holler is one thing cats do very well. In fact it often earns us shoes thrown in our direction, especially when the hollering takes place in the context of cat choir.

"You do realize we're totally going to miss cat choir, don't you?" said Harriet.

"I know, but this is more important," I said.

"I'm not so sure about that," she argued. "Odelia doesn't need us. She has Chase to look after her. Besides, what are we going to do when she's attacked by a zombie? Everyone knows zombies are dead people, and you can't protect yourself from dead people. All you can do is run."

"Or bash their heads in," said Brutus, who'd watched his share of zombie movies.

"Bash their heads in?" asked Dooley. "What do you mean, Brutus?"

"Well, zombies are operated by their brain stem, the most primal part of the brain, so if you bash their heads in, you make them fully dead, instead of just half dead." He leaned in, and added, "Their brain is where the virus lives—the virus that made them undead in the first place. So a well-aimed thunk on the noggin will take care of them."

"But... how are we going to deliver that well-aimed thunk on the noggin?" asked Dooley. "We're cats. We can't even get that high."

"Don't you worry about that part, Dooley," said Brutus. "Me and Chase got it all covered. All you have to do is play canary in the coal mine. Tweet if you see the zombie."

"Tweet if I see the..." Dooley muttered, thinking hard.

Brutus gave me a wink. "You, too, Max. Just be on the lookout for the zombie, and me my man Chase will take care of the rest."

"And how are you going to handle the zombie, exactly?" I asked,

"Don't you worry your pretty little head about that, Maxie baby," he said, puffing out his chest a little.

I rolled my eyes in response, and even Harriet seemed less than impressed by her mate's fighting spirit.

We finally arrived at the park, and walked the distance to the spot where apparently the altercation between Pamela Witherspoon and the zombie had taken place.

Chase quickly withdrew into the bushes that lined the road, and so did the rest of us. Odelia, of course, didn't have that luxury. She was the one acting as zombie bait.

Suddenly, Santa Claus came hurrying up, pulling on his red pants which were clearly too wide, and adjusting his white beard, which was a little ill-fitting, too.

"Alec!" Chase hissed from his bush. "Get over here!"

With surprising alacrity Santa Alec disappeared into the bushes.

"I'm sorry I'm late," he said. "Marge gave me a long lecture about the inappropriateness of our mother having another baby and I couldn't get away."

"Are you sure you being here is a good idea? You are

being suspected of assaulting a woman in this very spot, and here you are, returning to the scene of the crime."

"Pretty sure no one will recognize me," said Alec.

"You're dressed up as Santa Claus, Alec! You stick out like a sore thumb!"

"Yeah, I probably should have worn something a little less conspicuous," the former chief admitted. "Then again, like I said, no one will recognize me, and isn't that the main effect we're going for here?"

"The main effect is catching this zombie."

"Yeah, that, too."

"Maybe I could attend cat choir while you guys stake out the zombie," said Harriet now. "I mean, you don't really need me here, do you?"

"Maybe I'll attend cat choir too," said Dooley.

"Dooley!" I said, aghast. "You can't desert us. Odelia needs you. Uncle Alec needs you."

"I know, but I don't like zombies, Max," he said.

I sighed. "Fine. You and Harriet go to cat choir. Brutus and I will hold down the fort."

"You got that right, buddy," said Brutus.

We watched as Harriet and Dooley snuck off to cat choir.

"So how exactly are you going to bash that zombie's head in, Brutus?" I asked.

"Like I said, you don't have to worry about that," he grumbled. "I have my methods."

Brutus is butch, I have to admit. He's also a very strong cat. But he's no match for a zombie I didn't think.

Meanwhile, Alec and Chase were lurking in bush number one, so to speak, and Brutus and I were lurking in bush number two, while poor Odelia was resigned to stalking up and down the stretch of street lining the park. She was still uncomfortable in her outfit, but like a real trooper didn't let it stop her. And as she passed our bush for the third time in fifteen minutes, she whispered, "Still no sign of the zombie!"

"Are you sure it was here that Pamela met him?" asked Chase.

"Yeah, absolutely sure," said Uncle Alec. "He came up to her right here, and then she ran off, and bumped into me just around that corner over there."

"Maybe zombies aren't territorial," I suggested.

"Meaning?" asked Brutus.

"Meaning they don't stick to a well-defined area. Maybe our zombie is wandering Main Street right now, terrorizing people back there."

"We would have heard about that by now," said Brutus.

"Yes, Max," Odelia agreed. "If the zombie was showing his ugly face in some other part of town, we would have heard about it."

She decided to take another turn down the street, and teetered off on her high heels.

And just when I thought this stakeout was a bust, a car came careening down the street, and stopped right in front of us. Libby Elk came hopping out, followed by Jonah Zappa. They both joined us, totally giving away our position.

"Did we miss it?" Libby asked eagerly. "Did we miss the zombie?"

Chase emerged from his bush, looking annoyed. "Didn't I tell you to stay away, you two? This is a police operation, and you are potentially scaring off a suspect right now."

"I'm so sorry!" said Libby. "We'll hide in the bushes, just like you."

Chase returned to his bush, and Libby and Jonah occupied bush number three.

"So what's happening?" asked Libby, sounding excited about the prospect of witnessing a live zombie arrest.

"Nothing so far," said Uncle Alec. "And shouldn't you be filming my mom right now?"

"We have been filming your mom, but frankly it's getting a little tedious. I mean, she's already told us the story of her life. Twice. And we just thought we could combine two documentaries, one for Doctor Clam's clinic, and one about your zombies."

"So you guys work for this Doctor Clam?" asked Chase.

"No, we're both freelancers."

"We set up our own shop last year," said Jonah. "Before that, we worked for WLBC-9, but we got tired of waiting for better opportunities and better pay to come our way, so we decided to go into business for ourselves."

"So Doctor Clam is a client of yours," said Chase.

"Yeah, and a well-paying one, too."

"It's just that the subject matter is a little icky," Libby confessed. "He's made pushing back against the limits of nature his life's work. Only... I'm not entirely sure it's such a good idea for a woman of sixty or seventy to have a baby. By the time that baby is a teenager, his mom will be a very old lady."

"You shouldn't mess with nature is what I think," said Jonah. "Just look at these zombies. That's what you get when you start monkeying around with mother nature."

"You guys!" suddenly Odelia loud-whispered. "He's here! The zombie is here!"

We all glanced over, and I saw that she was right: the zombie had arrived, and was lumbering in her direction! And not only that, he had brought a friend!

13

*E*ven though the whole plan had been her idea, Odelia wasn't feeling entirely sure about its execution. It's one thing to devise a plan, but another to actually put yourself in harm's way. Besides, she was distinctly uncomfortable in her skimpy outfit. Even though Chase thought it was fantastic, and had already told her he hoped she'd wear it more often, she was feeling more than a little exposed. Especially when men were leaning out of their car windows to gawk at her. Lucky for her traffic was low this time of night.

And then there was the addition of Libby and Jonah, who no doubt were filming the whole thing. She had no idea what they hoped to accomplish but she did know she would hate to see herself on YouTube wearing these clothes.

And she'd just passed the bushes where her back-up team was ensconced, when suddenly she became aware of someone watching her. And when she abruptly turned, she discovered she was face to face with not one but two zombies!

They were leering, licking their lips, and stretching their arms in her direction!

She gulped, but instead of receiving the assistance she needed, exactly no one was jumping out of those bushes to apprehend those two zombies!

"Um, you guys," she said, raising her voice. "I could use some help here!"

The two zombies were grinning, their dead eyes flashing with delight.

She yelled a startled cry, and then teetered in the other direction. Their fingers twitching, they lumbered after her, moving a lot faster than she had anticipated.

She'd always thought zombies were slow, but these dudes were fast!

They absolutely looked the part, though: their faces were covered with open sores, their skin was veiny and almost translucent, peeling in places, and their hands were clawing the air like nobody's business. Yup. Zombies. Actual real-live zombies!

So she sped up, and was now drawing even with Chase and Alec's bushes again.

"Guys!" she said. "Now would be a good time!"

And as one man, the two cops finally sprang from their hiding place and accosted the zombies, who were completely taken by surprise. But instead of complying, one of the zombies hauled off and smacked Chase on the nose, while the other kicked Alec's shin.

Chase reeled back, and Uncle Alec danced a one-legged jig. The upshot was that when Odelia looked up, the two zombies were gone! Vanished into thin air, like a pair of ghosts.

"I'll be damned," said Libby as she, too, emerged from her bush. "Did you see that?"

"Yes, I saw that, Libby," said Odelia, disappointed by this mission failure.

"Where are they?" asked Chase, sufficiently recovered to ask a pertinent question.

"They went that way," said Jonah, his camera still pointing in the direction the zombies had disappeared. He now swung it right into Odelia's face. She pushed it away. She was not in the mood for cameras being directed anywhere near her person.

She looked in the direction indicated, but there was no sign of the zombies.

"Can you walk?" asked Chase in a nasally voice and still clutching his nose.

"Yeah, yeah," said Odelia's uncle, looking both annoyed and embarrassed.

"Chase, you're bleeding!" said Odelia, who only now noticed that her boyfriend had blood all over his face and shirt.

"It's fine," he said. "I don't think it's broken."

"Why didn't you give chase?" asked Uncle Alec.

"With these shoes?" she said.

"Well, you have to admit the plan worked," said Chase, holding a tissue to his bleeding and damaged snout. "Pamela got one zombie, you got two."

"And we got the whole thing on tape!" said Libby triumphantly. "So if you post this, we can prove that what the Chief and this Pamela Witherspoon person said was true: There are zombies in Hampton Cove, and they're attacking innocent women at night!"

"Now if only we could catch them," said Alec. He'd lost his beard somehow.

"Hey, weirdo!" a man driving past yelled. "Got lost on your way to the North Pole?"

A Coke can came sailing in Uncle Alec's direction and hit

him right in the chest. Coke splashed everywhere, ruining his nice Santa suit.

"Hey!" he shouted, but the guy was already gone, the car speeding up and turning a corner, tires screeching. "No respect," he muttered as he wiped the Coke from his suit.

Odelia sighed. "Well, I guess we better call it a night, you guys." She glanced down, expecting to see Max and Brutus. She frowned. "Where are my cats?"

"Oh, I think they went after the zombies," said Libby now.

"What?"

"Yeah, I saw them chase the zombies."

This night just kept getting better and better. Not!

14

---

*T*he moment those zombies started running, Brutus gave me a poke in the ribs, and yelled, "Let's go, go, go!" and then we were running, too.

Unfortunately cats aren't really built for marathons, more for sprints, and so by the time we came to the end of the street, I was completely exhausted. Brutus, who's more fit than I am, was still going well. Though, he, too, was clearly feeling the strain.

Lucky for us, the zombies must have experienced the same thing, for they had slowed down, and were now lumbering like before, arms outstretched, and staggering along the street. And then they disappeared into the park.

"Let's follow them at a distance," Brutus suggested.

"I thought you wanted to smash their brains in with your secret weapon?" I said.

"Okay. I might as well tell you now. I had actually planned to jump on top of the zombie's head and dig my claws into his temples, penetrating his brain and rendering it useless. At that point the zombie would simply fall to the ground. Only I hadn't counted on there being two zombies instead of just the one. It kinda ruined my super plan."

"I don't think you can actually reach into a person's brains by digging your claws into their temples, though," I said. "Your claws are too short to reach optimum penetration."

"Yeah, you're probably right," he said. "I guess I need bigger claws."

"You could try by simply digging your claws into their eyes," I suggested. "That way they won't see where they're going, and will be a lot easier to catch."

"Humans tend to protect their eyes, though," he said. "So that might not work either."

I had to admit Brutus was making a lot of sense when he talked zombie-fighting strategy like this. Then again, brute force is his hallmark.

"So what do you think about Grandma Muffin having another baby?" I asked.

"I don't like it, Max," he confessed. "It's going to create a lot of trouble for everyone involved. First off, Gran may think she's as fit as a twenty-five-year-old but she's not, so who's going to end up having to take care of that baby? Marge and Tex. And I don't think that's fair on them."

I stared at the cat. Often I see Brutus as an airhead bully, but today he was on fire.

"I agree with you wholeheartedly," I said therefore.

"Yeah, and also, that baby is going to attract a lot of attention. In fact that baby will soak up attention like a sponge. And where will that leave us? They'll neglect us, Max."

"That's what I'm afraid of. Though I'm sure Odelia would never let it come to that."

"Oh, yes, she will. Just you wait and see. Once that baby is born, they'll forget we even exist, and then we'll go days without having our food bowls replenished, our litter boxes cleaned out, and even for our water bowls to be filled with fresh water from the tap. We'll be fending for ourselves, Max, and I'm not sure I like that particular prospect."

I hadn't really thought about it that way, but I could see he had a point. Between work and taking care of a baby, our humans' attention would be on the baby, not cats.

Not a fun prospect!

We'd ventured deeply into the park by then, the zombies still lumbering on, with no obvious destination in mind.

"I wonder where they're going," I said.

"Maybe back to the graveyard?" said Brutus. "That's where zombies live, you know."

"I'm sure these are not really zombies. They're simply two men who look like zombies. Either they're dressed up as the walking dead, or they're really sick people."

Brutus considered this, then said, "Nah. They're zombies and they need their heads bashed in."

We were crawling through the undergrowth and the zombies were making a beeline for the beach. Hampton Cove park isn't all that far from the beach, and judging from the way they were going, they were looking to go for a nice refreshing swim.

"I hope they're not going in the water," said Brutus, following the same line of thought. "I can't swim."

"Neither can I," I admitted.

We were out of the park now, and had arrived on the boardwalk, but instead of stopping to take in the sights, the zombies staggered down onto the beach proper and moved in the direction of the ocean, whose waves were gently lapping the sandy beach.

We were still following along, though with less and less enthusiasm.

"They're going in, Max," said Brutus. "They're going to take a swim!"

And so they were. Both zombies had reached the water-line and stumbled in, the water soon reaching their knees and still they weren't stopping.

Brutus and I had stopped short of getting our paws wet, though. We're all for accomplishing our missions, but we draw the line at getting wet.

So we watched on as both zombies waded out farther and farther, and soon were lost from view.

"Do you think they'll drown?" I asked.

"Moot point, Max. Zombies are already dead."

"Touché."

And as we started the long trek back to the park, I glanced over my shoulder. The full moon cast its pale light across a peaceful ocean, but of the two zombies there was no trace. They'd been swallowed up by the waves.

And this mystery had just become a little mysteriouser.

15

*L*ater that night, when Odelia had finally returned home, she and the others were greeted by an irate Grandma Muffin, standing out on the porch.

"You took my camera crew!" the old lady cried, shaking her balled fist. "That's my camera crew and you took em!"

"Um, actually we volunteered," said Libby. "We couldn't resist filming a zombie, and we did!"

"Two zombies," said Jonah, holding up two fingers in case his meaning wasn't clear.

"Who cares about some stupid zombies! You have to be here, with me, all the time! That was the deal!"

"But you're not even pregnant yet," said Libby. "There's exactly nothing to film."

"Nothing to film? You have to film me!"

Libby gave her a confused smile. Clearly she wasn't all that happy with her assignment. "We can't film you all the time, Vesta. That's not how it works. We outline certain key scenes, and we film those."

"Yeah, if we have to film you every minute of every day, we're going to have a lot of wasted footage," Jonah agreed.

"Wasted footage? How dare you talk about my life as wasted footage! Every minute of every day is an important minute, and a minute people at home will want to watch!"

"People at home? We're filming a promo video for Clam's clinic," said Libby. "The only people who'll see this video are Doctor Clam's prospective clients."

"Wait, what? I thought this was a reality show," said Gran, looking even more dismayed now. "Like the Kardashians? Only about the Pooles, and most importantly, about me!"

"No, this is definitely not a reality show," said Libby. "And even if it was, they don't film the Kardashians all the time. That show is scripted, like all reality shows are."

Jonah nodded. "It's a common misconception. People think everything they see actually happened, but it's all scripted and staged, just like a TV show or a movie."

"What? No!" said Gran, looking absolutely appalled. "It's all real. We're all flies on the wall while those lovely Kardashians lead their lovely perfect lives in sunny California."

"That's not how it works," said Jonah. "And like we said, this is not a reality show."

"Yeah, this is not Keeping Up With The Pooles," said Libby.

Gran's shoulders slumped. She looked as if the wind had been knocked out of her. "No way," she said. "You cheated me. You told me…"

"I'm going to bed," said Jonah, yawning.

"Yeah, me too," said Libby. "I'm beat. I didn't know hunting zombies was so tiring."

And both disappeared into the house next door. Now it was just Odelia and Gran. Odelia felt for her grandmother. Even though she still thought the whole pregnancy thing was a crazy idea, it was obvious the old lady was very attached to the scheme.

"They're still filming you, Gran," she said. "And they're still making a video about you. And you're still having a baby. Isn't that the most important thing of all?"

"Yeah, but what good is having a baby if nobody is going to see it on prime time television?" She shrugged. "But like you said, I'll still have the tot. I guess I can parade her up and down Main Street for the entire town to see. Oldest mom in the world."

And then she walked in and closed the door.

Odelia decided it was time for her to hit the hay as well. She was still a little worried about her cats, but figured they'd be fine. They always landed on their feet, and she had no reason to think that this time would be different. She just hoped they hadn't actually tried to catch those zombies all by themselves.

When she walked into the kitchen she found Chase waiting there for her with two cups of hot milk. He handed her one.

She smiled as she took it. "Thanks," she said. "I needed that."

"So what do you think of that footage?"

Jonah had shown them some of the footage he'd shot of the zombies, but she didn't know what to make of it. "They could be actors and this whole thing could be a hoax," she said as she took a seat at the kitchen counter.

"Yeah, but why go to all this trouble, attacking people on the street?"

"Did you recognize them?"

"Nope. You?"

She shook her head. Of course it would be very hard to recognize anyone. The zombies' faces looked really ravaged and beyond any recognition.

"They didn't ring any bells with your uncle either."

"I wonder, though, Chase. Could they be... real zombies?"

73

He laughed. "Not you, too, babe. There's no such thing as zombies."

"Yeah, I know, but they looked so real. And so scary."

"I think these are two very confused men, suffering from some horrible, disfiguring disease, and hopefully for them we'll catch them soon, so we can take them to a hospital."

"My boyfriend. Always the voice of reason," she said as she smiled up at him.

"There's no other explanation that makes sense," he said, and leaned in to give her a kiss. "I'm bushed. I'm turning in."

"Me, too," she said. "Have our guests gone up already?"

"Yeah. Lucky for them we didn't throw out that spare mattress."

They'd recently turned the guest bedroom into a home gym slash office, but had kept a mattress just in case Gran fell out with Mom and Dad again and decided to bunk at her granddaughter's place.

"I'm glad Jonah managed to get those zombies on tape," said Chase, getting up. "If you post that video on the *Gazette* website, all this nonsense about Alec will finally stop."

"I hope so. Gossip is tricky, though. It might find a way to explain away the video."

But she hoped he was right, and that soon this whole ordeal would be over.

*C*at choir was in full swing by the time Brutus and I arrived back in the park. The playground, which cat choir's director Shanille has picked as its official rehearsal spot, is occupied by kids during the daytime, and cats during the night. Harriet was singing one of her famous solos when we took a seat and watched. I have to admit my mind was still filled with images of those two zombies walking into the ocean and vanishing without a trace, but obviously Brutus's focus was on his mate. She smiled when she saw us arrive, and I like to think her voice got that extra bit of pep that makes all the difference.

"Hey, Max," said Dooley, sidling up to me. "So how did it go? Did you catch the zombies? Did Brutus smash their brains in with his secret weapon?"

"No, we didn't catch them. We followed them all the way down to the beach, and then they went for a swim and didn't come back."

"They went for a swim? Is that typical zombie behavior?" he asked.

"I'm not sure," I admitted. "I don't really know all that much about zombies."

"Me neither. They don't typically feature on the Discovery Channel."

The Discovery Channel has become Dooley's station of choice lately. He used to watch a lot of the Hallmark Channel, but apparently Marge has switched allegiances, and now watches a lot of nature documentaries instead. Or maybe it was Tex.

"At least they didn't harm Odelia," I said. "They came for her, you know, and tried to grab her, but she was too quick. And then when Chase and Uncle Alec sprang from the bushes, they ran like the wind."

"I didn't even know zombies could run," he intimated.

We listened as Harriet sang a nice aria from some opera only she was aware of, and were joined by Shanille. "Is it true what I've heard about your uncle Alec behaving like a savage beast yesterday?" she asked.

"No, none of that is true," I assured her.

"It was the zombies," said Dooley helpfully. "It's all their fault. But now they've gone for a swim and we don't know when they'll be back."

"Okay," said Shanille after a pregnant pause. "So I overheard Father Reilly discuss Uncle Alec with some of his parishioners, and he's promised them to stage an intervention. He assured them that sex addiction is just like any other addiction, and he's convinced that if Alec joins the twelve-step program he can be healed. He'll also need to pray a lot, and he's going to invite him to come to church every day so they can pray together. He said Alec's soul can still be saved, but he will have to work, and work hard."

"I'm not sure Uncle Alec is going to like that," I said. "He's not a big churchgoer, I don't think."

"Well, he better start going now, or else he'll get kicked

out of Hampton Cove. People are talking about going over to his house and bodily grabbing him and banishing him from their town, telling him never to come back. Father Reilly managed to calm them down, but if he doesn't comply he will get banished. And I don't think he'll like that."

"No, in that case I think he'll definitely prefer the prayer thing."

Harriet was still singing her aria, and suddenly broke off and yelled, "Will you two stop yapping and pay attention to me for a second! Show some respect to your diva!"

So we shut up and paid attention.

She was right, of course. You ignore a diva at your peril.

❧

*A*lec arrived home after his stakeout, and was feeling pretty good. After all, with the footage of the zombies that this Jonah fellow had shot, and Pamela's statement, no one in their right mind could still claim he was a menace to society and women walking the streets alone at night, with or without dogs named Boomer.

And then he saw the car sitting in his driveway, a black-clad man leaning against it.

For a moment, he thought it was Chase, having come over for a quick chat before calling it a night. But then he saw that it was none other than Father Reilly, of all people.

What the…

He parked his truck right behind the priest's sedan and got out.

"Father Reilly? What brings you out here in the middle of the night?"

The priest smiled a beatific smile. "Alec. Just the man I wanted to see." He then let his eyes drop to the Santa costume the Chief was still wearing. "Fancy dress party?"

"No, a stakeout," he said. "We caught the zombies on film, father, so this whole ordeal of mine will soon be over."

"About that, Alec," said the priest, placing a hand on the Chief's shoulder. "I wanted to have a word with you. Some concerns have been raised about your recent behavior, and I would very much like to address them."

"Now? It's two o'clock in the morning, father."

"He who watches over us never slumbers or sleeps and neither does His servant," said the priest in kindly tones. "My flock asked me to convey an urgent message to you and I feel this cannot wait until the morrow. They are concerned, Alec. Very concerned."

"Well, they don't need to be concerned, father. Like I said, we got the zombies on film, and—"

"Myes. The thing is, there are a lot of women feeling very scared right now, and a lot of husbands, fathers, brothers and sons feeling very angry. In fact it isn't an exaggeration to say that you are not a popular man at this moment. People want you to leave town, Alec," he said sternly when Alec started sputtering something. "They want you gone. They want to organize what is commonly termed a mob and expel you from their town. I managed to convince them to give you one more chance—one last chance. And I hope you will grasp this chance with both hands, Alec," he added as he grasped Alec's hands and squeezed them tightly. "Do you see now why this couldn't wait until the morning?"

He felt a little deflated. "Um… they want to kick me out of town? But why?"

The priest smiled a sad smile. "Denial. I see this all the time. You, my son, have an affliction, and that affliction is an addiction. Not to booze or drugs, no, but something even more pernicious and vile. You, my son, are addicted to sex. And as you can clearly see, it's only getting worse," he said, raising his voice as Alec tried to get a word in edgeways.

"Admit you have a problem. Only then can the healing finally begin."

"But father—the zombies—"

"Shush, my son. I've decided to take you under my wing. I see now that I've been neglecting you for far too long. We're going to pray together, and this requires you to come to church for the liturgy of the hours. We will pray eight times daily, and you will attend mass every day as well. You will soak up your religion, son, and ask for forgiveness for the sins you have committed. Is that understood?"

"Um…"

"Is that understood?" said the priest, suddenly adopting a stentorian tone.

"Yes, father," said Alec meekly.

"You will also join my Monday evening AA group."

"But I don't drink—well, not all that much, anyway."

"If I had a nickel for every alcoholic who told me they don't drink, I'd be as rich as Jeff Bezos. So are you going to accept help and be healed?"

"Yes, father," said Alec, feeling like he didn't have much of a choice here.

"Good. With the Lord's help, I know we can beat this demon. Now let's go inside and pray."

"What, now?"

"Matins, Alec. Our two o'clock prayer. We'll also pray together for Lauds, Prime, Terce, Sext, None, Vespers and Compline. Do you own a Bible, Alec?"

"Um…"

"You can have mine," said the priest as he spirited a Bible out of thin air. "Read it, cover to cover, and then read it again. And again." Father Reilly now glanced up and read the message spray-painted across the garage door, then shook his head sadly. "See what we're dealing with here? This is the work of the devil."

"The work of Flint Dibbert and that no-good scummy little friend of his Bart Stupes, you mean," Alec muttered, but the priest was already walking up to the front door.

So Alec let himself in with his key, and led the holy man into the living room, where Father Reilly proceeded to balance a large cross on the living room table, then knelt down and told Alec to follow suit.

Five minutes later, Alec was praying alongside the priest, mainly for this whole ordeal to soon be over.

Whatever in hell had he done to deserve this?

17

*T*hat night when we came home, we were met with a fascinating sight: in Marge and Tex's backyard Gran was… dancing.

At first I have to admit I thought she was a zombie, but upon closer inspection I discovered it was actually our very own human, doing some variety of rain dance. She had her eyes closed and was dressed in a white flannel nightgown which was flapping around her bony ankles, while engaged in a frantic jig in place.

When I asked, "Gran, are you feeling all right?" she opened her eyes and stared at me, as if seeing me for the very first time.

Then, finally, she said, "Oh, hey, Max. I'm doing a fertility dance."

I stared at her. "Fertility dance?"

Dooley, who'd come up behind me, asked, "What is a fertility dance, Max?"

"I guess it's a dance to boost one's fertility," I said, though to be honest I was a little stumped myself.

"Doctor Clam told me to perform this ritual every night.

He says that the ancient tribes living in the Amazon Rainforest perform this ritual in the weeks and months before their anticipated mating date, and it never fails to work wonders."

"So... when is your... mating date?" I asked, though I wasn't entirely sure I even wanted to know.

"No date scheduled yet," she said, scratching her nose. "Doctor Clam has promised me the scouting process is going ahead as planned."

"Scouting process?" asked Dooley.

Harriet and Brutus had now also joined us, and the four of us stood watching the spectacle with no small amount of bewilderment, for Gran had resumed her jig.

"If I tell you, you have to promise me not to breathe a word about this to the others, you hear?"

"Our lips are sealed, Gran," I said.

"Okay, well, as you can imagine Doctor Clam has a lot of contacts in Hollywood, seeing as how he's the world's greatest fertility expert. So he's promised me the best male specimen to father my child. We're thinking George or Brad, or even one of the Chrises. But this is all strictly hush-hush, you hear? We feel that a specimen of the highest quality is necessary, plus, they'll get a lot of free publicity out of this. I mean, who doesn't want to be the father of the oldest woman in the world's baby? Huh? Right?"

I could have told her no one would want that dubious honor, but figured I'd better keep my mouth shut, as she had suggested. Besides, what did I know? Humans are weird, as I think we've established by now, and this was simply another case in point.

"That's great, Gran," I said therefore. "And I hope you get the best baby daddy in the world."

"I'm secretly hoping for one of the four Chrises," she said, a little breathless now after all that dancing. "Or maybe a cocktail of all four would be nice. Though to be absolutely honest with you, I'd much rather do this the good old-fashioned way, but Doctor Clam claims that's not practical. And since he's the expert, I'm going to follow his advice."

A window had opened on the second floor of the house, and Tex's head came poking out. "Vesta, what the hell are you doing down there?" he asked in slightly offended tone. All this dancing and yapping apparently was keeping him up.

"Put in your earplugs and shut up," she snapped. "Can't you see I'm in the middle of something?"

"In the middle of what?"

"I'm doing a fertility dance, to help me get ready for the big day."

"Fertility dance?" He looked just as dumbfounded as we did.

"It's a scientific procedure that's beyond your pay grade, Tex. Now leave me alone."

Shaking his head, Tex's head retracted and the window closed again.

Next door, Rufus, Marcie and Ted Trapper's sheepdog, had been alerted by the back-and-forth, and now peered over the fence. When he saw Gran perform her ancient Amazonian ritual, he tilted up his head and started howling like a timber wolf.

"Hey, it's working," said Gran. "That old dog is getting good and horny already."

Beyond Odelia's backyard, another dog had woken up: Fifi, Kurt Mayfield's Yorkshire Terrier, had slipped under the fence, and had now joined us. And as Rufus's howls intensified, the little Yorkie also threw her head back and joined the chorus. Soon all the dogs in the neighborhood had started howling, and since we didn't have much else to do, the four of us decided to raise our voices in song, too. We had just come from a cat choir rehearsal, so we were definitely in the mood for some more singing.

Windows were opened left and right now, and loud cursing filled the night air.

When Odelia's head appeared, looking sleepy, she asked, "What are you guys doing?"

"We're providing backing vocals for the dogs," I explained.

Only now did she catch sight of her grandmother, who was still doing her weird ritualistic dance, as envisioned by her fertility guru, and her jaw dropped a few inches.

"Oh, hell," finally Gran said when Tex returned, this time joined by Marge, and also Chase was staring at her, and Marcie and Ted Trapper, and of course Kurt Mayfield. Clearly she didn't enjoy an audience, for she shouted, "Fine! Tomorrow night I'll do it in the park, where no one will bother me!" And with these words, she hiked up her nightgown and returned indoors.

"What was that?" asked Ted from next door.

"I have no idea," said Marge.

"It's a fertility dance," said Tex. "She wants to become pregnant and this is her way of getting ready for the big day."

"Pregnant? But isn't your mother like a hundred years old or something?" asked Marcie.

"Seventy-five, and she hired a fertility expert," said Marge.

"She's nuts," was Kurt's determination. "Can we finally go back to sleep now?"

"I think it's cute," said Odelia.

Two more heads had come poking out. They belonged to Libby and Jonah, the latter hoisting his camera on his shoulder. I don't think I'd ever seen him without his camera, and I was starting to believe the thing was attached to his body somehow.

"So what did we miss?" asked Libby with a big yawn.

"Some old lady was doing a fertility dance," said Kurt. "It looked totally ridiculous."

"I thought it looked cute," Odelia repeated.

"So where is she?" asked Jonah, swinging his camera here and there.

"She went in," said Marcie. "I think she didn't care for all the attention."

"Too bad," said Libby. "So can you ask her to come out again? We need to get this on tape."

"You ask her," said Tex. "I don't have a death wish."

"Is she really going to have a baby?" asked Marcie. "I thought that was physically impossible?"

"Nothing is physically impossible in this day and age," said Marge. "If they can put a man on the moon, or even Mars, they can probably get my mother pregnant again."

"Hey, that's great news, Marge," said Marcie. "You're going to have a little brother or sister soon."

But Marge didn't look all that happy with the impending family expansion. Shaking her head, she disappeared from view.

"I have the impression your wife isn't all that happy about this, Tex," said Ted.

"You can say that again," said Tex, but refrained from adding any more comment. It was, after all, a very delicate matter.

Soon all humans had returned indoors, and the only ones still out and about were the felines and canines of Hampton Cove.

It's hard for a dog to stop howling once he's gotten started, and so for a long time after the lights had gone out and the houses had turned dark, they just kept on howling.

"They should probably start a dog choir," said Harriet after a while. "They're pretty good."

"I think cat choir is enough for one town," said Brutus. "Besides, who wants to listen to dogs yowling night after night? Not me."

"Not me, either, "I agreed.

The truth of the matter is that dogs are very one-note in their performance, whereas cats put a lot more variety in their act. Then again, I may be prejudiced. But I don't think so.

Soon, all was quiet again in Harrington Street, and we could finally get some sleep.

All but the zombies, of course, who were probably still lumbering away, now on the bottom of the ocean, trying to reach England. Well, good luck and good riddance.

18

The next morning, very early, Odelia's phone rang. Still groggy, she picked it from the nightstand, and saw that an unknown number was trying to reach her. As a reporter, she was used to unknown numbers trying to reach her, so she dutifully picked up with a reasonably cheerful, "Hello, this is Odelia Poole?"

"Hi, Miss Poole!" a very chipper woman's voice tooted in her ear. "I'm very happy to announce that you have been selected to participate in the Peppard Pet Food Miracle Cure test program! When can you drop by with your sweet and cute furry friends?"

"Oh, that's great," she said, rubbing the sleep from her eyes. "I guess I could drop by today? That is to say, where are you guys located, exactly?"

When the woman gave her the address, Odelia realized that it was right outside Hampton Cove, which was convenient, as she'd feared the Peppard people were in another county or even a different state.

"Yeah, I can drop by this morning if you like," she said. And when Chase, who'd also woken up, gave her a questioning look, she mouthed Peppard Pet Food, and he grinned.

For some reason Chase found everything connected with Odelia's cat collection endlessly entertaining. And even though he couldn't understand cats the way she and Mom and Gran could, he was privy to their little secret, and thought it was just great.

"I'll pencil you in at ten, how does that sound to you, Miss Poole?" said the woman, still continuing happy-peppy.

"Yeah, that's great. Oh, wait, you do know I have four cats, right? I did mention that in my application, I think?"

"Yes, I have you down for four lovely fur-babies. See you at ten, Miss Poole!"

After she hung up, she directed a keen look at the foot of the bed, where two pairs of eyes had eagerly been studying her throughout the entire conversation.

"You're in," she said, not wanting to keep them in suspense any longer than necessary. "The Peppard Pet Food Company has selected you for their test program!"

"Oh, yay!" said Dooley, actually putting his paws in the air. Max even want so far as to do a little victory dance at the foot of the bed, which consisted of a slight shake of the butt and a circular motion of his hips. It wasn't as awkward as Gran's nocturnal fertility dance, but it was still fun to watch, and made Chase laugh out loud.

What a nice way to start the day, she thought. And she hoped it was a sign for more wonderful things to come.

There was a commotion in the corridor, and as she shared a look with Chase, they both said simultaneously, "We have guests."

Something she'd completely forgotten about.

So they both got up, and made their way into the corridor. Libby looked up when they arrived, and said plaintively,

"Jonah's been in there for ages, and he won't come out, and I really have to tinkle."

Chase knocked on the bathroom door. "Everything all right in there, buddy?" When no response came, he knocked again. "Jonah?"

"Yes?" said a voice from the stairs, and when they looked over, saw that Jonah wasn't in the bathroom at all, but coming up the stairs. He had a blush on his cheeks, and had clearly been out for a morning hike, hoisting his trusty camera on his shoulder as usual.

"Jonah!" said Libby, clasping a hand before her mouth. "But if you're here, who's in... there?"

They all looked at that bathroom door, which was locked, as Chase now ascertained by jiggling the handle.

Sounds could be heard from inside. Stumbling sounds. And when suddenly the knob turned and the door swung open, Odelia stifled a scream when she found herself looking into the face of a... zombie!

It was a female zombie this time, but she looked as zombieish as the two zombies she'd made the acquaintance of last night: bad skin, lots of sores, hair hanging loose and limp along a deeply ravaged face, eyes veiny and red-rimmed, and clothes very soiled.

The zombie merely stared at them, obviously as surprised and confused as they were, then broke into a lumbering sprint for the staircase, shoving Jonah out of the way with surprising force, and then proceeding to stomp noisily down the stairs.

"What the hell is going on?" Chase said, and made after the zombie.

Soon they were all in pursuit, Jonah looking excited about the prospect of getting some more zombie footage on film, and Odelia hoping that this time they'd actually be successful in catching the zombie and getting to the bottom of this baffling mystery.

She knew that zombies didn't exist, but then who were these people, and what were they doing all over Hampton Cove—and now even using her bathroom?!

The zombie had reached the ground floor, and was now making a beeline for the front door. And she would have made it if not for one of Odelia's cats' toys tripping her up and sending her flying. She landed on her belly with a thud, and stayed down. Within seconds, Chase was upon her, but instead of incapacitating her, as per police academy training and department regulations, instead he opted to keep a safe distance.

"Um… so how do we handle this?" he asked, clearly reluctant to put this hands on the zombie woman.

"I'd say we call an ambulance," said Libby. "This is obviously a very sick person."

"But if she's dead already," said Jonah, "doesn't that kinda defeat the purpose? I mean, she probably needs an undertaker, not a doctor, right?"

"I'll ask my dad," said Odelia, and raced out of the kitchen door and into her parents' backyard. Moments later she was storming into their bedroom, and rousing her folks.

"Dad," she said. "You have to come with me. We caught one of the zombies, and now we don't know what to do."

To his credit, Tex was out from under the sheets and putting on his slippers in seconds, and then he was following her down the stairs. "You caught a zombie? How?"

"She was in my bathroom," said Odelia.

"In your bathroom?"

"Yeah. No idea how she got there, but now she's downstairs, passed out on the floor, and we thought you'd better take a look, just in case she's contagious or something."

They walked back into her house and to Odelia's relief the woman was still there, lying on the floor.

"She must have hit her head," she explained when her dad knelt down next to her.

She glanced down at the toy the woman had tripped over. It was a mechanical mouse.

"This woman needs a hospital," said Dad finally. "She's in a very bad way."

Immediately Chase took out his phone and called an ambulance.

"So… is she dead?" asked Jonah.

"No, she's not," said Dad. "She's alive, though I don't know for how much longer."

"So she's not a zombie?" asked Jonah, sounding disappointed. He was filming the whole thing.

"A zombie? No, of course not," said Dad. "She's a sick woman, and until I run some more tests I honestly have no idea what made her this way."

They all stared down at the poor woman, and Odelia felt relieved at her dad's words. "Not a zombie," she said, and Chase nodded curtly, as if to say, 'See? What did I tell you?'

"Man, what a bummer," said Jonah.

*D*ooley and I had followed the capture of the so-called zombie with rapt attention, and I had to admit I was as relieved as Odelia when the woman turned out not to be a zombie but an actual person. As I mentioned before, my knowledge of zombies is sketchy, but this seemed like a much better deal for all: no one's brains would get eaten, or smashed in, and now Uncle Alec was off the hook, too.

The ambulance arrived in due course, and even though the two paramedics frowned when confronted with their patient, they still acted like the professionals they were and put her on a stretcher and took her along to the nearest hospital.

Tex decided to ride in the ambulance with them, as his professional curiosity had been piqued, and since he wanted to know how the woman had ended up in his daughter's bathroom of all places.

And so when Harriet and Brutus finally wandered in, we had two wonderful bits of news to impart: the fact that we were going to have our first taste of Miracle Cure kibble very soon now, and that the zombies weren't zombies at all!

Brutus looked as disappointed as Jonah at the last part, but he soon recovered.

And when suddenly Gran walked in and demanded heatedly, "Where is my television crew? Have you been hogging my television crew again?" it was time for Odelia to put us in her car and we took off to the Peppard Pet Food Company.

"If the zombies aren't zombies, then what are they?" asked Dooley.

"I don't know, Dooley," Odelia admitted. "But I'm sure Dad will find out and tell us."

"I think Tex is wrong," said Brutus. "I think these are zombies, and soon they're going to wipe out the entire hospital, and then the entire town, and soon the whole world will become the setting for an army of walking dead."

"She's just a very sick woman," said Odelia. "And now she'll get the help she needs."

"Or she'll infect the doctors, the nurses, and everyone else in that hospital," said Brutus, who seemed to relish in his role as the herald of doom.

"Oh, nonsense," said Odelia. "She'll be fine."

"If she even makes it to the hospital," said Brutus. "She probably woke up during the drive, and first attacked Tex and then those two nurses before engineering her escape."

Odelia, even though logically she was inclined to refute this horror story, still picked out her phone and plugged it into her car's mobile phone connector, then called her dad.

"Dad? Oh, thank God. Is everything all right?"

"Well, the doctors here are a little baffled," his voice spoke over the car's sound system. "And frankly so am I. I've never seen anything like it. One thing's for sure: she's completely dehydrated and they're trying to get some fluids into her now."

"But what about her skin? She looks horrible."

"Yeah, she's suffering from some kind of rash," said Tex, and after telling her he needed to go, hung up.

"A rash," Harriet echoed. "That's putting it a little mildly, don't you think?"

"I still think she's going to infect this entire town," said Brutus. "She's probably patient zero, and soon they'll wish they never laid eyes on her. Mark my words."

"Oh, will you stop it, already?" said Harriet. "I'm sure the doctors at the hospital know what they're doing."

"It's a virus, Harriet," said Brutus. "Zombieism is a virus, and it spreads like wildfire. I just hope one thing."

"What?" asked Dooley, who'd listened to Brutus's exhortation with wide-eyed attention.

"That cats are immune to the disease. Even if humans all succumb to the horrible virus, I hope we will be spared."

"Let's talk about something more fun," Odelia suggested now. "How do you feel about the Peppard Pet Food Company, huh? Are you guys excited?"

We all yipped in acknowledgment, except Brutus, who was now somberly staring out the window, presumably on the lookout for the army of walking dead that soon would engulf the entire town.

"I hope we'll get to take some of the food home with us," said Dooley, clapping his paws excitedly.

"I'll bet we will," said Harriet. "How else are we going to enjoy the full experience? They have to give us a cat bag."

"I think the common term is doggie bag," said Odelia with a grin.

We'd arrived at the address indicated, and I saw it was located in a semi-industrial zone with other, similar low-slung buildings. Odelia drove up to the front door and parked the car.

As we set paw for the squat concrete structure, more

people drove up, escorting their pets, only they were all carrying their beloved animals inside pet carriers.

"We're the only ones not locked inside a cage," said Harriet, noticing the same thing.

"That's because you guys are all on your good behavior," said Odelia. Though as she glanced back at the other pet parents, she added, "Maybe I should have put you in pet carriers, too? Maybe this is some kind of policy they forgot to mention?"

"If that's the case, we might as well turn back right now," said Harriet. "I'm not going inside a cage for no one, not even for the Peppard Pet Food Company."

Odelia opened the door and we all streaked inside, our excitement undiminished.

The woman at the front desk smiled as she saw us tripping up to her, and after she'd ascertained that we were esteemed guests, pointed us in the direction of the welcome room, as she called it. As we entered Peppard Pet Food's Valhalla, I saw we'd arrived in the right place: the walls were covered with pictures of happy-looking pets, and dozens of other cats and dogs and even pet rabbits, hamsters, ferrets, guinea pigs and turtles were all waiting patiently with their humans, all looking equally exhilarated to finally find themselves in pet food paradise.

I was suddenly feeling like Charlie upon entering Willy Wonka's Chocolate Factory.

When Chase arrived at the precinct, he was surprised to see the reception area overrun with concerned citizens. Dolores was handling them with her usual flair and no-nonsense attitude, and when he joined her to see what was going on, she croaked, "Zombies, Chief Chase. Zombies everywhere."

"Zombies? You mean…"

"Yeah, all of these people have come to report zombie sightings, or even a zombie confrontation. Several found zombies in their bathrooms, or floating in their pools, and one even found a zombie in his jacuzzi. And let me tell you, they ain't happy about it."

Chase scratched his scalp. "So what happened with the zombies?"

"Some of them brought the zombies along," said Dolores, gesturing to an elderly gentleman with a resolute look on his face. "It's almost like a Take Your Zombie to Work Day. Kinnard!" she yelled. "Tell Chief Chase what you done did with your zombie!"

"Tied him up well and good, Chief Chase," said Kinnard, a

determined look on his wrinkly face. He ran the local liquor store, even though he looked old enough to have retired years ago. "Dumped his ass in the back of my truck. Ain't no zombies gonna eat me or mine!"

"Show me the zombie, Kinnard," said Chase, and followed the man out the door and into the parking lot.

And as Kinnard had indicated, the zombie was trussed up and lying in the bed of his truck. "He ain't going nowhere," announced the old man proudly.

"I think we better call an ambulance," said Chase. He glanced around at the parking lot, wondering if more people had followed Kinnard's example. And then he saw two zombies, also tied up and lying near the police station entrance. He hadn't seen them before, which meant they must have been delivered recently. He glanced around for a sign of UPS or FedEx but then caught sight of Wilbur Vickery entering the police station. He hollered, "Wilbur! Are those your zombies?"

Wilbur turned back and ambled up. "Yup, those be mine," he said good-naturedly. "Found them in my store fridge this morning, trying to crack open a can of Dr. Pepper. They were easy to catch, so I figured I'd better bring them over." He now glanced down into Kinnard's truck. "Will you look at that. More zombies."

"Yeah, looks like we've got ourselves a regular zombie invasion on our hands," Kinnard confirmed.

And as if to prove his point, suddenly a small army of walking dead now came staggering past. There were at least thirty of them, and they all moved unsteadily in the direction of Town Hall. And before the eyes of the stunned onlookers, one by one they all jumped into the fountain that had been erected in the middle of Town Square, and dunked themselves straight into the water.

"Well, I'll be damned," said Wilbur. "Those are some real

peculiar zombies."

"Most zombies eat brains, but these just want water," Kinnard agreed. He made a face. The owner of a liquor store, he wasn't partial to plain old water as a beverage.

He was right, Chase saw: the zombies were gulping up the water and really getting soaked.

He picked out his phone. "I better call the mayor. This is getting out of hand."

🐌

*C*harlene Butterwick had never in her wildest dreams expected her political career to start off with such a bang. She'd only ever harbored the ambition to go into politics to help her fellow townies and be of service to her community. She didn't want to become governor or president, just be the best mayor she could be. But she never thought she'd be faced with a zombie invasion her first week in office. So when she arrived for work that morning and saw a dozen zombies crawling all over the fountain in Town Square, with more arriving to join the party, she gulped and swerved and almost drove her car into the statue of a former mayor. Her phone chimed and when she picked up, saw that it was Chase, her brand-new chief of police.

"Um, Madam Mayor?" said Chase. "It would appear we have a zombie problem."

"I can see that," she said as she glanced over and saw Chase standing outside the police station holding up his hand.

She parked her car in her designated spot, got out, then quickly tripped over to where her chief stood.

"We caught one in my bathroom this morning," Chase said by way of introduction.

"And I caught one in my jacuzzi," said Kinnard, proudly pointing to the trussed-up zombie in his flatbed truck.

"And that's my haul over there," said Wilbur Vickery. "I found them having a go at a Dr. Pepper."

"The one we found in our bathroom is at the hospital right now," said Chase. "They're not actually zombies at all, but suffering from some kind of debilitating disease."

"Zombies are sick people, Chase, didn't anyone ever tell you that?" said Wilbur. "They're infected with some kind of virus, which makes them undead. So they're dead, but they're also not dead. And the virus is infectious. It spreads, so you gotta make sure they don't come near you, and especially that they don't bite you and eat your brains. That would be bad."

"This lot doesn't seem all that interested in brains, though," said Kinnard. "They like water."

"Yeah, they don't seem to go after other humans like most zombies do," Wilbur conceded. "But don't let that fool you. That doesn't mean they're not dangerous."

"What do you want to do, Madam Mayor?" asked Chase.

"Charlene, and I think we better call in some help. This is not something we can handle on our own."

"The FBI?" asked Wilbur.

"The FBI don't deal with zombies," said Kinnard. "You need to call in the army. They need to set up a perimeter and cordon off this whole town."

"Let me talk to the County Executive," said Charlene. "I'm sure there's a procedure we need to follow when dealing with this kind of thing."

Kinnard raised two very bristly eyebrows. "Well, good luck with that."

The chatter in the waiting room had become deafening. You can probably imagine how much noise dozens of cats, dogs, rabbits, hamsters and other pets can make, and when you add in the excited conversations of dozens of proud pet owners, a Metallica or Iron Maiden rock concert is probably the only thing that even remotely compares.

But when the doors of the room suddenly swung open and a man with a white mustache and white goatee appeared, the chatter died away and all eyes fastened on this remarkable apparition.

"Hi, my name is Fred Peppard, and I'm so happy to welcome you all to my program," the man intoned. He looked a little like Colonel Sanders. He then spread his arms wide. "Welcome, pets and pet parents, and let's all have some fun!"

Loud cheers rang out, and we followed the man into the next room. Well, at least Odelia and we did, and the dozen or so dogs present. The other pet parents all had to pick up their pet carriers and carry them over, which I thought was a little sad. Then again, it did provide Dooley, Brutus, Harriet and myself the opportunity to be the first ones to enter Fred Peppard's Pet Paradise. For that was what this clearly was: I could see pet toys everywhere, climbing poles, toy dog bones, and those dangly things more adventurous cats like to dangle from. But first and foremost, I could see large bags of pet food piled high, and all of them were labeled Miracle Cure.

"Oh, my," said Dooley, jumping up and down with anticipation. "Oh, my, oh, my, oh, my."

"This is looking good, you guys," said Brutus. "This is looking mighty good!"

"I just hope there's enough for everyone," said Harriet, sounding nervous. "I mean, look at the number of pets. They may have accepted too many applications and underestimated the response rate."

"Oh, relax, Harriet," I said. "Can't you see those bags? There's plenty for everyone."

But then I caught sight of some very big and very hungry-looking dogs, and I wondered if Harriet didn't have a point.

Fred Peppard soon put us at ease, though. "This is how this will work," he said, clapping his hands. "Every pet will go through a quick medical checkup to determine a baseline of health and fitness. Then we'll assign a certain amount of Peppard Pet Food Miracle Cure for them and they will eat this with relish, I can promise you. We'll repeat this during the three days they'll spend at our facility, at the end of which we'll repeat the physical, and see if there have been marked changes in their overall health and fitness levels, which I can also promise you there will be!"

"We have to get a physical?" asked Harriet, aghast.

"We have to stay here for three days?" asked Dooley, equally aghast.

"Yeah, they didn't mention that over the phone," said Odelia, also dismayed.

"If for any reason you feel like you can't in all good conscience leave your pet with us for the designated time span, that's just fine," Peppard continued. "You're free to leave right now, and grab yourself one complimentary bag of Miracle Cure as a thanks from us to you. If you do decide to enter your pets into the program… free pet food for life!"

"Free pet food for life!" Dooley cried, almost fainting from sheer excitement.

All around us, excited chattering broke out, as pets all across the room were already salivating at the prospect, and pet owners were already counting out their profits.

Odelia had crouched down and asked, earnestly, "Are you sure you want to go through with this? I don't care about this pet food for life scheme, all right? All I care about is seeing you guys happy and healthy and enjoying yourselves. So just say the word and we're out of here with our one bag of kibble."

"Four bags of kibble," said Brutus. "Four cats, four bags. Right?"

"I want to stay," said Harriet now. "Not for the pet food for life thing, but just look at all the friends we could make—the bonds for life we could forge by participating."

She didn't sound entirely sincere, I thought, but I decided to keep my tongue.

"Yeah, I want to stay, too," said Brutus. "I like the prospect of helping these nice Peppard Pet Food people to create the best pet food on the planet. I want to help."

Again, not entirely sincere.

"I don't like the idea of a physical, but I think I want to stay, too," said Dooley. "I like to eat, and I like to eat for free."

Now that was sincere.

"I guess I want to give it a shot as well," I finally intimated. "It looks like a nice experiment, and I'm sure they'll handle everything by the book."

"I don't know…" said Odelia, clearly of two minds about this.

"Look at it this way," I said. "You get to save a lot of money on pet food and we get to spend three days in pet paradise."

She smiled. "Well, if you put it that way… All right, fine. But on one condition."

"Anything!" said Harriet.

"I'll drop by tomorrow morning, and if you don't like it here, you tell me and I'll take you home. Deal?"

"Deal!" we all said, and put our paws against Odelia's hand for a high five.

And thus our Peppard Pet Food adventure finally began.

22

Alec opened his door carefully, hoping to avoid getting a brick against the noodle, but to his relief the coast was clear. So he stooped down to pick up his newspaper, and saw that someone had scribbled across the front page the words, 'Repist Go Ome!'

"I am home, you morons," he muttered, and turned to go in when a car honked and drove up his driveway. It was Father Reilly.

"Well?" said the priest, getting out. "Where were you this morning?"

"This morning?" he said, wondering what the old coot was talking about.

"Lauds! I was waiting for you at five o'clock!"

"Oh, damn," he said, earning himself a scowl from the priest. "I mean, shoot. I totally forgot to set my alarm clock." In actual fact he had no intention whatsoever to sit down with Father Reilly eight times a day to pray, and do daily mass and confession on top. He might as well join a convent, which actually was starting to sound like a pretty good idea.

"You made a promise to me and to yourself, Alec," said the priest, adopting a stern tone. "Not to mention to the Lord Jesus Christ who is Your Savior. Do you want to be healed or not? And, more important, do you want to have a future in this town or not?"

Alec rolled his eyes. "Look, I…"

But whatever he wanted to say was wiped from his lips when a curious sight suddenly arrested his attention: up and down the street a horde of zombies were staggering, followed by a horde of Hampton Covians, walking at a safe distance, carrying clubs and sticks, and clearly wondering what was going on, same way he was.

Father Reilly had turned and was now taking in the strange spectacle. "End times," he suddenly whispered. "The end times are upon us."

"It's zombies, father," said Alec. "Nothing to do with end times."

"Chief Alec!" one of the people passing by yelled. "You have to help us! These zombies are everywhere!"

"I'm not your chief anymore," he yelled, but still wondered what could be done about this sudden invasion of weirdos.

"Looks like we've got bigger fish to fry than Lauds, father," he said, and took out his phone.

When it connected, Chase immediately said, "We've got a big problem here, Alec."

"Yeah, I can see that. My street is being overrun by zombies. There must be at least two dozen of them."

"Same thing here. Mayor Butterwick has called the County Executive, who's called the Governor, who's called in the army. Let's hope they can contain this thing."

"What do you want me to do, Chase?"

"They don't seem to attack people right now," said Chase,

"but they are attracted to bodies of water. Still, I'd advise everyone to lock themselves up in their houses, make sure all doors and windows are fastened and secured, and sit tight." He sighed. "This thing is out of our hands, I'm afraid. Once the army gets here…"

"Yeah, it's over and out for us," said Alec. Chase disconnected, and Alec turned to Father Reilly. "You better go home, father. And pray that this will all be over soon."

But suddenly a zombie must have spotted them, for he came lumbering up at surprising speed.

"Father, watch out!" Alec yelled, and Father Reilly squealed and hid behind the former chief's broad back.

But instead of attacking them, the zombie dove into Alec's small fish pond instead!

"My koi!" Alec cried. "The nasty piece of work is going for my koi!"

Father Reilly, emerging from behind Alec, gulped a little, then said, wiping beads of sweat from his brow, "Maybe I will do as you suggest, my son. Go home and pray. And you better do the same thing. May God help us all." And then he practically jumped into his car, and led it careening out of the driveway and racing off, tires burning rubber.

❧

*V*esta, who didn't give a hoot about zombies, or the Peppard Pet Food Company, thought it was a disgrace. The biggest news in town should be her pregnancy, and now her thunder was being stolen by these stupid zombies and her cats wanting to eat some new kind of kibble. Not fair!

Her camera crew had taken off, presumably to go and film some more zombies, Odelia had disappeared, and so had

Marge and Tex. And when she approached Zebediah Clam, to ask him about the next step in her procedure, she found him watching TV, nervously biting his nails.

"More zombies," she said as she saw what he was watching. "Who cares, right?"

"The idiot," said the doctor. "The total, absolute moron."

"Look, Doc," said Vesta, who couldn't agree more. "I've been thinking, and I'm inclined to go with Chris Pratt. He's handsome, he's funny, he's talented. Any woman would be lucky to have his baby, and so I've decided to pick him. I mean, Chris Pine, Chris Hemsworth and Chris Evans are okay, but for my money I'm going to bet on him to deliver me a dream baby."

But to her surprise, Doc Clam wasn't even listening.

"The idiot!" he grunted as he watched the screen, where more zombies had taken to the streets, and were now walking in their typical lumbering gait. There was footage of zombies jumping into fountains, zombies jumping into the lake, zombies being dragged out of bathtubs and shower cabins, and even the local spa had reported having to pick zombies out of their sauna cabins. It was a regular invasion! And the frantic newscaster who kept yelling at the top of her voice didn't help either.

Vesta rolled her eyes, and raised her voice to drown out the annoying reporter. "Though if you want we could go with Clooney, of course. He's still a solid performer, though he's getting a bit long in the tooth now. Or how about Brad? Going strong, right?"

But the doctor didn't pay attention. Instead, he got up and said, "I gotta go."

"You mean to pick up Chris Pratt's sample? Can't you have it FedExed?"

But instead of responding, Doc Clam was hurrying out

the room, and moments later she heard the front door slam, and when she glanced through the window, saw his car backing out of the driveway and then race off with tires screaming.

She blinked. "So how about Alec Baldwin? He's local."

2 3

Odelia had finally left, and so had the other pet parents, and we'd all been allocated to different nurses' stations for our physicals.

Harriet, Brutus, Dooley and I had been placed outside nurses' station number five, along with half a dozen other pets, all of them cats. I saw from the lines at other stations that the Peppard Pet Food people had grouped us according to species: dogs together, rabbits together, hamsters, turtles...

Fortunately for us we knew all the cats lining up with us. They were all members of cat choir, obviously, and we had known them for years. Tigger was there, the plumber's cat, and so was Buster, the barber's cat, and Misty, the electrician's cat, and Missy, the landscaper's tabby, and Shadow, whose owner Franklin Beaver runs the hardware store. In fact I saw a lot of familiar faces in other lines, too. So maybe Harriet was right. This was a great opportunity to strengthen those eternal bonds of friendship.

"I'm so excited, you guys!" said Tigger. "Pet food for life! How great is that?"

"I'm not so sure about this physical, though," said Buster. "As a rule I don't like physicals. Each time Fido takes me to Vena, I puke. Literally puke all over the backseat. It's horrible. Though probably more horrible for Fido, as he has to clean it all up."

"Nobody likes Vena," said Brutus.

"Yeah, Vena is the worst," Missy agreed.

"Though you have to admit she knows her stuff," I said. "Last time I was there she fixed my teeth. I'm not one to sing her praises, as all veterinarians are evil, obviously."

"Obviously," my fellow felines echoed.

"But she did me a good turn there."

"I just hope they give me a clean bill of health," said Misty. "What if I don't get approved? What if I flunk the physical and they send me home empty-pawed!"

"They won't send you home," said Harriet. "This is just a formality."

"Yeah, they just want to establish a baseline of health and fitness," said Shadow, "so they can determine whether their pet food diet has made a difference after three days."

"Three days is not enough," said Brutus. "They should keep us here for three weeks, minimum. Then they'll be able to tell if their Miracle Cure makes a difference or not."

"But I don't want to stay here for three weeks," said Dooley.

"No, me neither," I admitted.

"Three weeks is too long," Misty agreed.

But then the line moved, and suddenly it was my turn!

I was grabbed by a very pleasantly plump young nurse who put me on a scale, then checked my teeth, listened to my heart and lungs, checked my paws, and proceeded to prod and poke me in places I really didn't like to be prodded and poked, except maybe by Odelia, and even then only on a good day. Still, I allowed her to do all this, as a big poster on the wall said, 'Miracle Cure: give your beloved pet the gift of life!'

Well, I don't know about you, but I enjoy life, and I would never say no to having more of it.

Finally the physical was over, and I was handed off to a matronly woman who grabbed me by the neck and unceremoniously carried me off, then stuck me... in a cage!

The door locked and I found myself staring at the iron bars of a real cage, just like the one at Vena's!

This wasn't part of the deal. I'd anticipated spending quality time in a playroom, enjoy a nice mani-pedi and watching others climb one of those climbing racks while I shot the breeze with my friends while gobbling up my body weight in Miracle Cure.

As I glanced around, I saw that I was in a room full of similar cages, over half of them occupied by equally-stunned-looking pets, who certainly hadn't signed up for this.

"Yelp," I said, hunkering down and tucking my tail around my buttocks in dismay. "Odelia, help!"

But of course Odelia was long gone.

Suddenly a big hatch opened in the cage's ceiling and something dropped down. It was kibble. The hatch closed again with a metallic sound, and as I stared at the small ration, I realized this was the famous Miracle Cure kibble. I licked one up and distributed it around my mouth, then grimaced and spat it out again. Yuck! It tasted like cardboard soaked in vinegar!

A noise alerted me of a presence nearby, and when I glanced over, I saw that a camera was carefully filming my every move.

I froze in my tracks as I stared into the lens. There was no cameraman, no Jonah Zappa handling the contraption.

Instead, it was mounted in the corner of my cage, swiveling while it registered my every single move.

Next to me, a cage door was opened, and Dooley was dumped in.

"Max!" he cried. "What's going on?"

"I think this is the Peppard Pet Food Program, Dooley," I said sadly. "We're test animals now. Guinea pigs. And whatever we do is filmed and presumably analyzed by the Peppard Pet Food people."

A hatch in his cage opened and a ration of kibble dumped in. And as he took a tentative sniff, his face contorted. "This is horrible. What is it?"

"Miracle Cure," I said. "Better don't eat it. It tastes horrible."

"But maybe it has all the essential nutrients and life-affirming vitamins your growing kitty needs?" he said, quoting from the commercial.

"I doubt it," I said, as I plunked myself down on the metal floor of my cage.

"They're not going to keep us in here for three days, are they, Max?" he asked. "That's not what it said in our contract, right?"

"What contract? I didn't sign no contract."

"We'll tell Odelia when she comes to visit us in the morning," he said. "We'll tell her and then she'll take us home and write a strongly-worded letter of complaint to Mr. Peppard. She could even write a front-page article about the way we're being treated."

He was right. The pet food people didn't know we could talk to our human, and so when Odelia showed up tomorrow morning to check on us, we'd blow the whistle on the pet food people and this would all be over.

So all we had to do was survive twenty-four hours in this horrible place and we'd be saved.

Soon we were joined by Brutus, Harriet, and the others. Harriet screamed bloody murder when she was tucked into her cage. The gang was complete, even though separated by iron bars.

"Twenty-four hours, you guys," I told them. "Just take a twenty-four-hour nap and when you wake up this will all be over."

At least I hoped so.

24

eturning from Peppard Pet Food headquarters, Odelia decided to drop by the hospital and see how her dad was doing with the zombie they'd found in her bathroom.

She called him on her way there. He said the zombie was in good hands, and was receiving all the medical attention she needed. The doctors hadn't figured out what was ailing her exactly, but they had determined she was suffering from extreme dehydration and was confused and disoriented, and couldn't speak or give them any indication who she was or how she'd gotten into this terrible state.

She arrived at the hospital and parked her car, then went in search of the ward where the woman was being treated, and soon discovered that whomever she asked about her grew a little shifty-eyed and evasive.

Finally she decided to check the ICU, where presumably she would have been taken, and found that no one would allow her to see the woman, or even acknowledge she was there.

And as she approached a doctor and asked him straight

114

out where the patient was, he said he wasn't at liberty to discuss the case with her and directed her to the hospital's director.

Starting to get a little hot under her collar, Odelia stalked over to the director's office and knocked on the door. She was admitted by a nice secretary, who said, when she heard why she was there, that the director wasn't giving any statements and told her to come back the next day.

"But... my dad was here. He worked with your staff!"

"I can neither confirm or deny that such a patient was ever admitted to this hospital," said the secretary, still in the same professional and friendly tones.

"Look, I'm the person who found the zombie—for lack of a better term—in her bathroom, all right? I called the ambulance that brought her here. I think I have a right to know what's going on." She was tapping the woman's desk with her index finger now, feeling a little annoyed about being given the runaround.

"Oh, I totally understand, Miss Poole," said the woman in the same unctuous tone she'd been using for the past five minutes, "but like I said, I can neither confirm or deny that a patient like the one you're describing has been admitted to our hospital. But I'm sure that if you put your request in writing, we will get back to you promptly."

"When? When will you get back to me?" she demanded.

"Promptly," repeated the woman with a smile.

She clearly wasn't getting anywhere, so she decided to leave it and do as the secretary suggested. Still, she had a feeling something very fishy was going on and she vowed to get to the bottom of it... promptly.

*a*t the library, Marge hadn't been able to attain her customary equanimity. The events of the previous day were still going through her mind, and she hadn't slept well. Not least because her mother had been keeping her up with her fertility dance, causing all the cats and dogs in the immediate vicinity of Harrington Street to break into an hour-long howling concert.

She was seated behind her desk now, hoping Alec was all right, but mostly wondering what this whole zombie thing was about. Her husband had called her from the hospital, saying it was the single most weirdest case he'd ever been involved with, and even the specialists at the hospital had been absolutely baffled.

The doors of the library swung open and Mrs. Samson walked in, carrying her usual shopping bag filled with romance novels to return. Marge didn't know how she did it, but she read at least five or six novels a day. Sometimes more.

Mrs. Samson now came walking up to the counter and deposited the novels in front of the librarian, then looked up and said, a little hesitantly. "I just want you to know that I don't believe a word they say about your brother Alec, Marge. Not one single word."

"Why, thank you, Margaret," she said. "That's very nice of you to say. And I'll be sure to tell Alec. He'll be so pleased."

Margaret adjusted her glasses and gave her an owlish look. "I mean, I can certainly imagine how a man of your brother's dimensions would have no trouble dragging Pamela Witherspoon into those bushes and overpowering her. Pinning her arms to the ground and having his way with her—ravaging her, so to speak. His lips on hers, his hands all over her body, ripping the buttons of her blouse while his tongue takes on a life of its own, plunging into her mouth over and over and over again…" She was breathing a little rapidly, her rheumy eyes glittering. "But like I said, I'm sure it never happened and Pamela is simply making it all up, like a wanton woman like her is wont to do."

"Yes," said Marge, as she confirmed that 'Primal Passion,' 'Hot Stud,' 'Take Me,' 'Barely a Lady,' 'Message From a Rogue' and 'A Billionaire's Virgin Capture' were checked in again. "Yes, I'm sure it's all a big misunderstanding and it will be cleared up very soon now. And then things will go back to normal again."

"That would certainly be very nice," said Mrs. Samson with a radiant smile, and shuffled off in the direction of the romance section for her haul of the day.

Marge shook her head as she watched the old lady move off, then was alerted by the sound of shouting outside. She got up from behind her desk and quickly made her way to the glass doors to look out. The sight that met her eyes was a very unusual one: a dozen zombies were tottering along the street, arms outstretched, fingers grasping the air, as they made a beeline for the decorative pond in front of the library.

One by one, they all plunged in, as if they'd never experienced water in their lives.

It was a horrifying sight, and Marge inadvertently held her hands to her face. Then, as one of the zombies' eyes fastened on hers, she quickly locked the library doors and backed away.

The zombie apocalypse had reached Hampton Cove, and now they were all in terrible, terrible danger!

"What's going on, Marge?" asked Mrs. Samson, but then she caught sight of the strange spectacle and said, "Oh." She blinked and adjusted her glasses. "Is that… an orgy?"

"We have to escape," said Brutus.

"No, we just have to wait for Odelia to show up," I said. "Which she will tomorrow morning, just like she promised, and then everything will be all right."

We'd been fed more kibble, but again it was mostly inedible, something I'm sure had been registered by that infernal camera.

A little hatch in the bottom of my cage had opened up and the excess kibble had all been removed and now my cage was kibble-free again. Which of course was not the way I liked it, but it was better than having to smell that horrible sour kibble.

Maybe they were making adjustments to their secret formula?

"I say we do as Max says," said Dooley now, my faithful friend.

"I'm not so sure, you guys," said Misty. "I think Odelia might show up tomorrow morning, as promised, and the pet food people will simply send her away with some excuse."

"Odelia would never accept any excuse not to see us," I

countered. "She'll barge her way in here and save us from these people for sure."

All around us, laments had been rising up now that we were complete, all the physicals over, a full contingent of test subjects ready to go. From time to time the laments were interspersed with some hatch being opened either to drop kibble in or out, but apart from that, not much had happened, and we hadn't seen a single human, and most certainly not Fred Peppard, who'd seemed so nice and welcoming before.

"How would we even escape?" asked Harriet now, who'd been refusing to lay down on what she deemed was a filthy cage floor but now finally succumbed to the temptation to take a load off her paws. "These cages look pretty sturdy, Brutus."

"The hatch," Brutus said, pointing at the hatch in the ceiling of his cage. "I'm sure Dooley could manage to wriggle through. He's tiny."

"I'm not tiny," said Dooley, a little indignant. Though he was staring at that hatch and clearly wondering if Brutus was right.

"Those hatches only open intermittently," I said. "Dooley would have to be very quick to launch himself through, and even then he might get stuck. And what happens if the hatch suddenly closes again?"

"I would be chopped in half!" Dooley cried.

"You wouldn't get chopped in half," said Brutus. "The worst that could happen is that you get stuck. Big deal."

"But I don't want to get stuck," said Dooley.

"Yeah, but look at the bright side," said Brutus. "If you succeed you could go and find Odelia and save us all. You'd be the hero, Dooley. And we'd all be very grateful."

"I could give it a shot," said Tigger. "I'm pretty small, too."

He was. Small and red. A little like me, though I'm big and blorange, of course.

"Look, even if this works, and either Dooley or Tigger manage to squeeze through, they're still going to be stuck in this room with no way out," said Harriet.

"I'm sure there's a way out," said Brutus. "And if there isn't all they have to do is wait until some human comes in and sneak out."

"No humans ever set foot in here," said Missy. "This seems to be some kind of self-contained system, fully-automated. Designed to operate without human interference."

"So what's going to happen if I have to wee-wee?" asked Misty. "I mean, I feel a wee-wee coming on just now, and I don't like to wee-wee without my litter box."

"Just wee-wee on the floor," said Buster.

"No way!" said Harriet, clearly horrified by this unsanitary notion.

"Where else are you going to wee-wee?" said Buster. "There is no other way."

"We could hold it in," said Harriet. "I think I can probably hold it in for twenty-four hours, until Odelia comes and saves us."

"Everyone knows that's not healthy, Harriet," I said. "Bad for your kidneys."

"Odelia should never have left us with these Peppard people," Brutus grumbled. "She should have done her due diligence instead of simply trusting that snake oil salesman."

"You believed the snake oil salesman," I pointed out.

"Yeah, but I'm a cat, she's a human. She's supposed to be smarter than me."

We all stared before us for a moment, thinking about our predicament, then suddenly I heard a tinkling sound followed by a satisfied little sigh. Misty had done her business and she clearly was relieved to have relieved herself. Then, after a beat, she said, "So now where do I sleep?"

All I could wonder was what would happen if I had to go number two.

Probably better not to go there.

❧

*F*ather Reilly was so glad to be back at his church that he clasped his hands together and raised his eyes heavenward to thank the Lord for looking out for him so very well.

He entered the church and walked along the nave when suddenly he thought he heard a sound. Almost like… a dog was lapping something up. It was dark inside the church, as he didn't like to switch on the lights unless strictly necessary.

He glanced around, and then heard that strange sound again. Water rippling.

And then he saw it: near the baptismal font, half a dozen zombies were wrestling each other to dive head-first into the font!

The sight was so gruesome and horrifying that for a moment he stood frozen to the spot, then howled a terrified scream and ran.

But even as he was running, he suddenly was filled with righteous indignation. This was the Lord's home! These zombies had no business defiling the House of Christ!

So he returned on his steps and picked up a chair and, screaming like a banshee, ran toward the feasting zombies while holding the chair aloft.

The zombies, though, if they were impressed by the on-storming priest, certainly didn't show it. They simply went on bathing and drinking from the holy water.

And even when the priest hit one of the zombies on the

head with the chair, the zombie merely shook his head and gave the priest a dirty look, then, as one zombie, they all stepped away from the baptismal font and began chasing after him!

And as he raced through his own church, he thought these zombies were a lot faster than Hollywood made you believe. Curse those Hollywood producers, he thought. They should have warned him that zombies could actually outrun their living counterparts!

Even before he'd reached the heavy oak doors, the zombie army had finally caught up with him and then they were all piling on top of him.

Yup. This was the end, all right.

Now he was going to turn into a zombie himself.

But instead, after roughing him up a little, they simply left him lying there and left.

So he just lay there for a moment, glancing up at the church ceiling. He saw Saint-Cecilia smiling down at him from her stained-glass window, and Saint-Joseph and even Saint-Peter. And as he waited for the transformation to take place, he soon realized no transformation was taking place at all.

And as he got up and dusted himself off and touched the black eye those ruffians had given him, he frowned. He fingered his face. No sores, no terrible skin. Nope. He hadn't turned into a zombie.

And then he smiled and sank down on his knees. "Thank you, God, for protecting me from the zombie apocalypse. Thank you for not allowing them to turn me into one of their own."

Praise the Lord. He'd been saved! It was nothing short of a miracle. And as a jubilant ecstasy suddenly filled him, he decided to spread the word. If he could be saved by his faith, so could others. And then he was off on his mission.

"*M*ax, look!"

I looked, and saw that Dooley had managed to open the hatch in his cage.

"It opened and so I thought I'd try to stick my paw in and it didn't close."

"Must be some sort of safety mechanism," I said. "To prevent pets from getting hurt. Can you pass through?"

He stuck his head in and easily slipped through and was now on top of his cage.

"Yay," he said. "I escaped!"

"Well done, Dooley," I said.

"Now you try, Max. It's easy. You start with your head, and the rest just follows."

I wasn't absolutely convinced of the wisdom of his words. Dooley is easily half my size, or even less, and that hatch didn't look all that big to me.

"I'll give it a shot," said Tigger, and within moments he was out, too. Soon the others all followed suit, and even Harriet and Brutus managed to sneak through that hatch without a hitch.

They were all encouraging me to give it a shot, but unfortunately things had gone wrong from the first. I'd managed to pry open the hatch but the moment I put my head in I'd gotten stuck, and there was no way I was able to perform the rare feat they'd all pulled off with such practiced ease.

"You go on without me, you guys," I said. "Get out of here and tell Odelia to come rescue me, will you?"

"Just a little push, Max," said Harriet, as she grabbed hold of my head and tugged.

Brutus now joined in the escape attempt and tried to pry my head loose from its parent body.

"Ouch," I said. "Easy with the claws."

"How else can I get purchase?" he asked, quite reasonably too, I thought. Still, I could do without the acupuncture session.

In the end they had to admit defeat. My head might have gotten through all right, but the rest of my body refused to follow.

"I don't understand," said Dooley. "When your head fits, the rest should fit, too. That's the rule."

"Well, I guess I just broke the rule," I said.

"It's because Max has a weird body shape," said Brutus. "His head is smaller than the rest of his body."

"Look, just go," I said. "I'll be fine."

"It's not his head that's small," said Harriet. "His head is quite big."

"I didn't say his head was small," said Brutus. "I said it's smaller than the rest."

They stared down at me. "Mh," said Harriet. "I think the problem is his gut."

"Just go already!" I said, not comfortable being objectified like this.

"We're not leaving you, Max," said Harriet.

"You have to leave me," I said. "I'll be all right. I have

plenty of food and water, and knowing you're all safe and sound will get me through this ordeal."

I'd managed to retract my head and was back inside my little cage, while my friends debated their next course of action. Finally they had to agree that leaving me behind was probably the best option.

"We'll come back for you," said Dooley, as he reached a paw into my cage and I touched mine against his. "I don't like this, Max. I don't like leaving you behind."

"It's just for a little while," I said. "Now you go and get help. I'll be right here waiting."

Of course I was. What else was I going to do?

And then they were off, watched by dozens of pets. More pets had managed to squeeze through the hatches, but only the smaller ones. The big ones, like yours truly, were well and truly stuck, and would remain that way until the cavalry would show up in the form of Odelia.

I just hoped they wouldn't be long, as I was starting to get a little claustrophobic in my temporary lodgings.

❦

"*I* really don't like leaving him behind," Dooley repeated. "I really don't. Isn't there something we can do to get him out of there?"

"Not unless you have a way of unlocking those cages, Dooley," said Harriet.

"There has to be a way to get that mechanism to snap open," said Brutus. "Maybe there's a control room or something? A way to open those cages remotely?"

The large warehouse-type space where the cages were located was indeed monitored, with a camera in every cage. So it surprised Dooley that no one had dropped by to stop their escape attempt. Maybe no one was watching? Or the guard keeping an eye on them had gone for a bathroom break? Whatever the case, they had managed to get this far, and now all they needed to do was get out of the building and find their way home.

The small troupe of pets proceeded in the direction of a large bay door that was, of course, closed.

"There must be a button we can push," Tigger said as they studied the door. It was enormous, and reached all the way to the ceiling, high and wide enough to allow a trailer to back up to be unloaded. And then Dooley saw it: there was indeed a large red button, only it had been installed at a convenient height for humans, not pets.

"There," he said. "I'll bet that button opens this door."

They all looked where he was pointing, and agreed that in all likelihood that button was *the* button.

"But how to reach there?" asked Harriet.

"Can any of you jump that high?" asked Misty.

Unfortunately the pets in their present company were the smallest of the bunch. Brutus was, in fact, the biggest, but even he couldn't jump that high.

"Maybe we can form a pyramid," Missy now suggested. "We all stand on top of one another and the one on top should be able to push that button."

"So who's going to be at the bottom?" asked Brutus. They all stared at him, so he grumbled. "All right. I guess I'll be at the bottom of this pet pyramid."

"I guess me, too," said Buster, who was a wiry but powerfully built cat, like Brutus.

So while Brutus and Buster braced themselves, the others all jumped on top, and soon formed a feline pyramid. Dooley was the last one to climb the furry pile of cats, and when he reached the top, sitting squarely on top of Harriet's shoulders, he managed to reach the button and tap it!

There was a whirring sound, and the bay door started to roll open.

"We did it!" said Dooley. "Max would be so proud!"

They all watched as the door inched open, then slid underneath it and found themselves outside. They'd made it: they'd escaped Peppard's Pet Paradise unscathed!

Suddenly they were surrounded by a group of men dressed in blue coveralls, all armed with nets. And before they knew what was happening, they'd been caught in the nets. A man materialized before them. Dooley recognized him as Fred Peppard himself.

"Well done, you guys," he said. "Initiative, cooperation, derring-do. You just qualified yourselves for the next round of my experiment. You are, without a doubt, the nimblest and smartest of the bunch, and as a reward you get to enjoy the latest addition to the Peppard Pet Food Company's nutrition program: Miracle Cure II, new and improved!"

And with a nod of the head, he gestured for his men to take the escapees back inside.

Oh, no, Dooley thought. It looked they'd just landed themselves in a real pickle. And the worst part: he and his best friend were now separated. He so did not like this!

*A*s Odelia exited the hospital she took out her phone and rang her dad. Oddly enough she couldn't reach him, as the call went straight to voicemail. She then tried to reach Chase, but the same thing happened: no response.

Odd, she thought, but figured they were both busy.

And she'd just gotten into her pickup when suddenly what looked like a military truck blocked her exit and two soldiers jumped out, approached her and yanked open the car door.

"Please come with us, Miss Poole," said one of the military men.

"Why? What's going on?" she asked, greatly surprised.

"I'm sorry," said the soldier, "but those are my orders. Please come now."

She glanced in the direction of the hospital, and saw the secretary watching on from behind her office window. All she could think was that she must have called in these soldiers.

"Am I under arrest or something?" she asked.

"Please, Miss Poole," said the soldier. "Don't make this

harder than it needs to be." And he grabbed her by the arm to bodily remove her from the vehicle.

So she decided she better do as he said, and followed along. Taking her place inside the military jeep, she was quickly whisked away.

𝕔

*C*hase was in Chief Alec's office, which apparently was now his office, discussing the recent events with Charlene, when suddenly two soldiers burst in. They were both armed and looked like they meant business.

"Chief Kingsley? Mayor Butterwick? Please come with us, madam, sir."

"What's going on?" asked Charlene. "Where are you taking us?"

"For your own safety, you have to come with us," said the soldier.

His colleague was more forthcoming. "The whole town is being evacuated, Madam Mayor. The entire population will be in quarantine for the unforeseeable future, and our orders are to take you to a temporary camp that's being set up on the town perimeter."

"You're evacuating the whole town?" asked Chase. "Isn't that a little… extreme?"

"We have no idea what we're dealing with as of yet, Chief," said the soldier. "So just to be on the safe side we're locking down Hampton Cove. Now please come with us."

And as they followed the two soldiers, Chase saw that all of his colleagues were undergoing the same fate: all of them were being escorted out of the building, and into waiting military trucks, to be taken to a destination unknown.

Dozens of trucks were parked along the road, and people were escorted inside by military personnel. Some people went willingly and gladly, others put up a fight. Resistance was futile, though, and eventually everyone was loaded onto the trucks.

"I don't believe this," said Charlene, once they were seated. "They could have told me what they were planning. I'm still the mayor, for crying out loud."

"And I'm supposed to be the chief and they kept me out of the loop, too," said Chase.

The military had taken over, and the civilian authorities had been shut down.

Chase took out his phone to call Odelia, but the moment he got it out, one of the soldiers snatched it from his hands. "No phones," he said sternly, and pocketed the phone.

"But I want to call my girlfriend," he said. "To know if she's all right."

But the soldier merely held out a hand for the Mayor to deliver her phone, too. Wordlessly, she handed it over.

Moments later, they were roaring away.

෫෧

*M*arge was glad she was safe inside the library, but wondered how long those zombies would keep frolicking in her pond. She hoped they'd finally get tired and move on, but so far they didn't give any indication of that.

And as she was watching on, a military truck suddenly stopped in front of the library, and men dressed in hazmat suits suddenly got down and approached the zombies. The men were all wearing protective masks and were armed. As they got closer to the zombies, they got down on one knee, raised their weapons, aimed, and fired!

The zombies all dropped down, and only now did Marge see that no bullets were used but darts of some kind.

130

"Tranquilizer shots," said Mrs. Samson, who'd been following the entire sequence from the safety of the library, same as Marge. "They use it to tranquilize wild animals, and zombies, I suppose." She glanced out at the people in the hazmat suits, who now carried the zombies to the truck, loaded them all up and moved on.

"Do you think they'll come for us, too?" asked Marge.

And her words were still hanging in the air when a second truck stopped and two soldiers hopped down, then approached the library.

Marge quickly unlocked the door. "Thank God," she said. "Thank you so much for getting rid of those terrible zombies. I didn't dare open the door."

"How many people inside the library, ma'am?" asked the first soldier, who looked young and buff and very authoritative.

"Just me and Margaret," said Marge. "I had to close my doors because of the zombies."

"Are you going to take us, young man?" asked Margaret now.

"Yes, ma'am, I am. Please come with us."

"Oh, with pleasure," said Margaret, well pleased.

"Where are you taking us?" asked Marge, a little surprised.

"They're taking us to their barracks, of course," said Margaret. "To do with as they please. That's what nice soldier boys do to innocent women such as ourselves."

"We're simply going to put you in a safe place, ma'am," said the soldier.

"Are you going to be there, young man?" asked Margaret as she held out her arm and the young soldier complied by hooking his arm through hers and escorting her out.

"Yes, as a matter of fact I am."

"Ooh," said Margaret, then suddenly stumbled. The young

131

soldier effortlessly scooped her up and carried her off to his truck. She was pleased as punch. "Why, you're so strong," she cooed, touching his bicep appreciatively. "Do you have a girlfriend?"

Moments later, the truck was off, and so were they.

"I like this, Marge," said Margaret. "I like being abducted by these nice young men."

Marge was happy for Margaret, though she wasn't as relaxed about this so-called abduction as Margaret obviously was. She had a feeling this was not an abduction she was going to enjoy.

*A*nother portion of kibble was being dumped into my temporary home, but I didn't even pay it any mind. Even from the smell I could already surmise I wasn't going to like it. I had a feeling they kept trying different types of kibble, in the hopes they'd get some takers, but from what I could see, no one was even taking so much as a nibble.

Obviously they still had a long way to go to perfect their Miracle Cure kibble, and we were the hapless pets chosen to test their inferior product.

At least Dooley and the others had all managed to escape, and were now presumably on their way home, to warn Odelia of what was going on here.

I'd briefly wondered about those cameras, though. What's the point of having a camera in every cage if you're not going to watch the feeds and notice half a dozen cats escaping, along with a couple of rabbits and a bunch of hamsters and guinea pigs?

I'd plunked down on the floor of my cage, and was now staring through the bars, waiting for my rescue party to finally show up.

They'd come any moment now—I simply knew they would.

*D*ooley and the others had all been taken into a large space, a little less cavernous than the warehouse they'd been kept in before, and once again had been locked up in a set of cages, albeit considerably roomier than the last ones.

"I think we've just been upgraded," said Harriet, who was clearly gratified to see that in the corner of her new cage a patch of litter had been placed where she could do her business.

"So they were monitoring us," said Brutus. "They watched our every move, and anticipated our escape."

"Yeah, it would appear so," said Tigger sadly.

A helping of kibble had dropped down into Dooley's cage and he took a tentative sniff. It didn't even smell half bad, so he took a provisory nibble.

"Yum," he said. "You have to try this new kibble. It's tasty."

"I'm not hungry," said Harriet. "All this captivity has made me lose my appetite. I think I'm developing Stockholm Syndrome."

"Stockholm Syndrome means you start getting attached to your captors," said Missy. "Have you fallen madly in love with Fred Peppard, Harriet?"

"Um, not exactly," she said.

"I think it's PTSD," said Shadow. "We're all suffering from PTSD now. And probably will have to visit a shrink for the rest of our lives to deal with this terrible trauma."

"No, I mean it's really good, you guys," said Dooley, as he gobbled up some more kibble. "I think we did the right thing by escaping. At least now they're feeding us something edible."

"So what is this place, exactly?" asked Brutus. "Some kind of psychological experiment?"

"I don't know and I don't care," said Harriet. "All I care about is getting out of here." She glanced up at the hatch through which the kibble dropped into their prison cell. "These hatches are a lot smaller than the ones in our previous cells."

"Yeah, this time there's no escape," said Misty sadly.

"Almost like they wanted us to escape before," said Shadow.

"I wonder what they want us to do this time," said Brutus. He shoved against the bars of the cage but they didn't budge. "Pretty solid steel cages. No way of escape this time."

"No, but they're really, really good," said Dooley. "Just try. You won't be disappointed."

"Oh, can you stop eating already, Dooley," said Harriet. "You make me sick with your constant chewing."

Dooley abruptly stopped chewing, and swallowed the kibble whole. It was okay. He didn't have to chew. He could simply gobble them down. "Yum," he muttered. He might not have managed to escape, but there had been a marked improvement in their conditions, which was progress as far as he was concerned. He just felt for Max, who was still having to eat that nasty kibble. It wasn't fair, he felt. It wasn't as if Max wasn't smart enough to escape, or fit enough. He was simply big-boned. And that wasn't his fault.

So whoever was behind this whole thing clearly wasn't fair. Otherwise they'd have allowed Max to escape, too, and they could have enjoyed this nice kibble together.

*G*ran had decided to head down to the office. At first she'd figured that throughout her entire pregnancy she'd better stay home and rest, but since losing her camera crew, and her doctor, she was bored. Besides, it wasn't as if she was pregnant yet. Chris still had to send in his sample, and then Doc Clam had to do whatever it was that he did.

So she grabbed her purse and stepped out. It was only a short brisk walk to the heart of town, where Tex's doctor's office was located, and the fresh air would do her good. She'd taken a nap after Doc Clam's sudden departure, her earplugs in and her eye mask on, and was feeling thoroughly refreshed.

It was probably those hormone cocktails Clam had been giving her. They made her feel fit as a fiddle. If she kept this up, she'd live to be a hundred-and-fifty, and she now wondered if Clam hadn't merely unlocked the secrets of fertility, but also of eternal life.

As she walked down the street, she was surprised to find the streets completely deserted, not a single soul in sight.

No people, kids or even mothers pushing their strollers.

She frowned as she passed the park, and saw that even there no one was around. Usually some kids could be found playing in the playground, their mothers sitting on the nearby benches busily tapping on their phones, but today there was absolutely no one.

She didn't even see any cats or dogs, which was also unusual.

She shrugged. Probably all busy someplace else.

She arrived at the office and walked in, loudly yelling, "Tex! I'm here!"

When her son-in-law didn't immediately respond, she shoved open the door to the inner office and found that he wasn't behind his desk, or examining a patient. In fact there were no patients, either, and the phone wasn't ringing off the hook as it usually did.

Huh. Weird. Tex wasn't one to play truant. The man had his faults—many, many, many of them, in fact—but tardiness wasn't one.

She took a seat behind her desk and booted up the computer, then proceeded to play Solitaire for half an hour, after which time she was bored out of her skull again, and decided that if Tex couldn't be bothered to show up for work, she didn't have to, either.

So she grabbed her coat and purse and walked out again.

The day was sunny and bright, and a little stroll through town would do her good. She could do some shopping and then return home for another nap. Doc Clam had told her she needed to nap a lot, as those hormone cocktails were some heavy-duty stuff.

But as she reached Main Street she was surprised to find all the shops closed, and not a single person on the streets.

Huh. Creepy. Had someone decided to close down the town and neglected to tell her?

And then she saw it: a military vehicle had been parked in the middle of Main Street, and a soldier now descended. He was pointing a rifle in her direction, and said, "Zombie, desist!"

"What did you just call me?" she demanded heatedly.

"Frank, I found another zombie!" he yelled to what she assumed was his buddy.

"Well, just shoot it and get it over with it," a voice sounded from inside the Humvee.

The soldier then aimed, and actually pulled the trigger!

She felt a projectile pass by her left ear, and shook her fist. "Hey, are you nuts? Aim that toy gun at some other joker, will you?"

"The zombie is still walking, Frank. I repeat, the zombie is still walking."

"That's because you shoot for shit. Let me have a whack at it," said the disembodied voice, and then a second soldier appeared, also holding a rifle. He aimed at her, and shot!

Another projectile whizzed past her right ear, and this time she thought that maybe, just maybe, it wouldn't be such a bad idea to make a run for it.

So run she did!

hen Odelia arrived at the camp, she was surprised to find that there were already hundreds, perhaps even thousands of people present. She saw tents, large and small, she saw soldiers patrolling everywhere, and she saw people she recognized as Hampton Covians standing huddled together, talking amongst themselves, and clearly wondering what was going on, same as she was. And just as she got out of the truck and was escorted past the fence and into the camp, another truck arrived, and her mom got off!

"Mom!" she cried, and joined her mother, who looked confused and disoriented.

"What's *happening?*" asked Marge.

"Thank you so much, young man," said Mrs. Samson as she was helped off the truck by a soldier.

"This has probably something to do with the zombie thing," said Odelia. "The army must have decided to put the entire town in quarantine."

"But why? We're not zombies."

"They don't know that, do they? And besides, with every

virus there's an incubation period where you're not really sick yet, even though you already have the disease."

"I don't feel sick," said Mrs. Samson. "In fact I've never felt better in my life."

"Yeah, I don't feel sick either," said Marge. "And I haven't even been in contact with any zombies."

"No, but I have, and you've been in contact with me, so potentially we could both have been infected."

"I wasn't infected," said Mrs. Samson. "I would remember if a zombie had his way with me."

"So why bring us here?" asked Marge. "Why not simply tell us all to stay home and not leave the house?"

"They have a better chance of containing the disease this way," said Odelia. "And I'll bet they will have rounded up the zombies, too, and put them in a different camp."

"Yeah, I saw how they shot the zombies with tranquilizer guns," said Marge.

"See? I think it will all be fine, Mom. They know what they're doing," said Odelia, as she hugged her mom. "This is all a little scary, but it won't be long before we're home again."

"I don't want to go home," said Mrs. Samson, glancing at the soldiers. "I like it here."

More trucks arrived at the entrance to the camp, and one of the people getting off was Chase. Odelia smiled as he walked up to her, and they hugged. She noticed Mayor Butterwick had been picked up, too, and wondered where the rest of her family could be.

"So they got you, too, huh?" said Odelia.

"Yeah, a little surprising, as I'm supposed to be chief of police now."

"I guess civilian rank doesn't have any meaning anymore," said Marge.

"They probably declared a state of emergency," said

140

Chase, "and took over the entire town to prevent the disease —if that's what this is—from spreading any further."

"Have you seen Tex?" asked Marge now. "Or Alec? Or my mother?"

"No, I'm afraid not," said Chase.

"I tried to call Dad but he didn't pick up. And then they took away my phone."

"Same thing here," Chase grunted.

"I'm worried about my cats," said Odelia now. "They're still in that Peppard Pet Food place, and I promised to visit them tomorrow, but I don't think this will be over by tomorrow."

"No, I doubt it," said Chase. "I have a feeling we might be here for a couple of days or even weeks."

They glanced around at their new accommodations. "Looks like we'll be living in tents for the time being," said Marge.

"Oh, goodie," said Mrs. Samson. "I love camping. It's so exciting. You never know who might drop by your tent in the middle of the night." And she set off in the direction of the nearest tent to check it out.

"Well, at least someone is enjoying herself," said Chase with a smile.

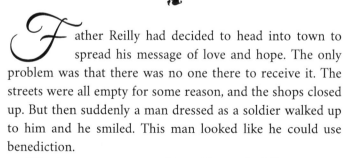

Father Reilly had decided to head into town to spread his message of love and hope. The only problem was that there was no one there to receive it. The streets were all empty for some reason, and the shops closed up. But then suddenly a man dressed as a soldier walked up to him and he smiled. This man looked like he could use benediction.

"Blessings to you, my son," he said warmly. "The answer is

prayer. Pray and ask forgiveness for your sins and all will be well. And you'll see that the Lord's Benediction will wash over you like a warm bath and his love will heal you and save you from harm."

The soldier, who was a young man, didn't appear to be very responsive to the lessons Father Reilly tried to impart. On the contrary, he was eyeing him a little suspiciously, and barked, "Not one step further, sir. Stay right there."

"Brotherly love is what we all share, son," said Father Reilly. "Brotherly love. It's the gift that keeps on giving. Let me wrap you in the Lord's embrace and share his message."

"Sir, I'm warning you," said the soldier. "Not one step closer."

"I just want to give you a hug," said the priest, holding out his arms and stepping up to the young man. "Let's celebrate His love and hug it out. Share that brotherly love."

But instead of brotherly love, the soldier pointed a weapon at him. There was a short puffing sound and when Father Reilly looked down at his abdomen, he saw that some kind of dart had been fired at him, and it was now stuck in his belly.

Almost immediately he started feeling weak-kneed, and then he was falling to the ground. The pavement rose up with surprising speed and smacked him in the face.

Oh, not again, he thought, as his eyes closed. And then he was lost to the world.

❦

*A*lec, who'd decided to return indoors and wait out this annoying zombie invasion, had been reading his morning paper, his feet up on his coffee table, and was thinking that a man could get used to this kind of life. Maybe the Mayor had done him a good turn when she'd suspended him and told him to go home and stay there for the time being.

He'd worked his entire adult life in the service of Hampton Cove, until Hampton Cove had spat him out over some unsubstantiated piece of gossip. So maybe he should take the hint and officially announce his retirement?

He could even move south, and start a new life down in Florida. Though he doubted whether his pension would stretch as far as that.

Then again, he could open a camping site down there and rent to snowbirds.

And he'd just decided to take a nap when there was a loud knock on his front door.

"Not again," he muttered, figuring it was those annoying neighborhood kids again, or some old harridan come to call him names.

So he decided to pretend he wasn't home. After all, they couldn't look in through his window as he'd replaced it with a piece of chipboard. When he heard a noise at the back, and saw someone trying to glance in through the window, he quickly ducked down.

After a while he figured the coast was clear, so he closed his eyes and went to sleep. After the night he'd had, he deserved a nice little nap. And soon he was dozing peacefully.

ou may or may not be aware of this, but cats have a great fondness for taking extended naps. In fact when we have nothing to do, we simply curl up into a ball and nap away to our heart's content, which is what I'd been doing since my friends had escaped. I was awakened now by the sound of a click, and when I glanced over I saw that my cage had been opened. I didn't waste time, therefore, to push it open further, and taste some of that sweet and delicious freedom I'd been missing.

Oddly enough mine was the only cage that had malfunctioned in this way, for the other pets were all still confined to their cages, most of them having followed my example and taking a nap.

I decided that somehow Dooley and my friends had managed to free me—perhaps they'd discovered the control room from where our cages were being monitored, and had pushed the right button corresponding with my particular cell and had released me.

I was certainly grateful, though I now wondered where I had to go to find the elusive exit to this place.

I decided to follow in my friends' pawsteps, and headed for that big bay door I'd seen them open with their feline pyramid. Clever bit of thinking, I'd thought at the time, and even though I was all by myself, and it's hard to form a feline pyramid by your lonesome, I figured I'd think of something.

I stared up at that big red button and wondered how I was ever going to reach there when I got an idea. Cats can jump pretty high, but they can jump even higher when they take a running leap. What if I simply ran up to the button, and jumped as high as I possibly could?

So I gave it my best shot. I took a running leap at the thing and got liftoff, sailing as high as I could, my paw reaching out to hit that darn button.

Unfortunately I'm one of those cats that are built for comfort, not speed, or even height, so I didn't actually manage to hit my target.

But I was undeterred, and decided to give it another shot. The second time I flew in a little lower than the first time, and the third time I missed the button by a wide margin. And so I sat, puffing and panting, and looking up at that button, my holy grail.

And I would probably have gone for a fourth attempt when I suddenly saw an old chair lying in a corner of the warehouse. So I shambled over and gave it a tentative kick with my paw. It didn't look like much, but it just might do the trick.

I dragged it over as best I could, then managed to put it upright. Jumping on top of it was but the work of a moment, and when I stood on my tippy-toes and reached as high as I could, stretching the old spine... I finally managed to slam that sucker!

The gate responded with pleasant alacrity, and then I was hopping down from the chair, giving it a fist bump in gratitude, and sliding under the door and into the open air, which felt like a balm. And I'd just opened my mouth and was taking in big gulps of refreshing oxygen, when a big man with a white goatee walked up to me and arrested my progress—and sense of jubilation.

"Well done, fat cat," said the man, whom I now recognized as Fred Peppard himself. "I knew I could count on you to show me something truly remarkable. As a reward for a splendid performance you can now join test group number two."

He gestured with his head, which at first I thought was a nervous tick, and the same woman I'd made the acquaintance of before grabbed me by the neck and carried me away.

So much for my Herculean efforts to escape!

I was carted off into another, smaller room, and locked up in a bigger cage. But this time I was relieved when I suddenly heard familiar voices welcoming me into their midst: Dooley, Harriet and Brutus, and of course the rest of our cat choir contingent, were all there to greet me!

We were reunited. And still prisoners of Fred Peppard's creepy Pet Food Company.

"How did you make it out of there, Max?" asked Dooley excitedly.

"I thought you guys did that," I said honestly. "My cell door suddenly clicked open and I thought you'd somehow managed to hit some button somewhere and release me."

"No, we didn't hit any buttons," said Harriet.

"We have been twiddling our thumbs a lot in here," said Brutus. "But I don't think that counts as staging a rescue attempt."

"What is this place?" I asked, as I glanced around. Whereas the other cage I'd been held in was located inside a large warehouse, this was just a plain room, one wall consisting entirely of cages, and several small gates located in the opposite wall.

146

"I have no idea," said Dooley, "but the kibble in here is much better than the kibble in our old place. Here. Have a taste." And he flicked a piece of kibble in my direction.

I caught it open-mouthed and munched it down. Dooley was right. This stuff was a lot tastier than the previous stuff. "Yum," I said. So Peppard was capable of creating cat kibble after all.

"So if we manage to escape again we'll get even better kibble you think Dooley?" asked Shadow.

"Yeah, I'll bet we do," said Dooley. "Each time we escape, conditions improve. Unfortunately," he added, "there doesn't seem to be a way to escape this new prison."

I'd immediately noticed that the cages were more sturdy, of better design, and the opening through which kibble dropped in small enough only to allow a rodent to pass through. And cats may be many things, but we're definitely not rodents.

Suddenly, there was a clicking sound, followed by another clicking sound, and I noticed how both mine and Brutus's cages had suddenly been opened. We tentatively pawed them open further, then walked out.

"Hey, not fair!" said Harriet as she shoved against her own cage. "How did you do that?"

"I didn't do anything," I intimated. "It opened by itself."

"Someone is playing games with us, Max," said Brutus. "And I'm not sure I like it."

He was right. We were being played by an unseen hand, though I had an idea the hand belonged to a man with a goatee whose image was on all Peppard pet products.

Suddenly the six little gates across the room swung open, and different objects appeared: four were plastic flowers, and the fifth and sixth were plastic rabbits.

Brutus glanced in my direction. "I have a feeling they want us to go after the rabbits, Max."

"Yeah, too easy," I conceded.

"So maybe do as they want? Or try the flowers instead?"

"I guess we better do as they say," I said. "And then maybe we'll get another reward."

"Hey, don't leave us here!" said Harriet. "Brutus, snuggle bug! Don't leave me!"

"I'm not leaving you, snuggle pooh. I'm simply trying to get out of here so I can get help," said Brutus, as he approached his mate and they shared a quick cuddle.

"I'll be back," I promised my friends.

"I know you will, Max!" said Dooley. "Go get them, tiger!"

And so Brutus and I both set paw for the respective rabbits.

We were literally going down a rabbit hole...

31

---

*V*esta had run into an alleyway. She didn't mind soldiers but she did mind being shot at. When she looked back, she saw they were hot in pursuit, so she decided to hide in one of the dumpsters. With some effort, she managed to clamber into one, and settled in for the duration. The thing was stinking something real foul, but at least she was safe.

What was happening to this town? Zombies chasing innocent women all around the park at night, soldiers taking potshots at senior citizens, and people running off and disappearing on her for no good reason!

"Wait till I tell my son," she murmured. "He'll throw you lot in jail so fast!"

The dumpster suddenly opened and someone peered in. But Vesta had taken the precaution of hiding underneath some pizza boxes and soon the dumpster closed again.

"Not in here!" the man shouted.

"Pass along," Vesta muttered. "Nothing to see here."

She waited a while longer, and then decided that the coast was probably clear by now, and carefully lifted the dumpster lid to peer out. Glancing left, then right, she saw that she was all alone in the alleyway, and climbed out of her hiding place.

"What are you doing?" suddenly asked a voice from underneath the dumpster. She was startled, but quickly recovered when she discovered the voice belonged to an old friend of the family: Clarice. The feral cat was munching on a fishbone and gave Vesta a curious look. She looked as ratty and mangy as usual, but at least she wasn't equipped with a gun and wouldn't try and shoot her.

"Am I glad to see you," said Vesta, getting down and taking a seat. "Some guys dressed as soldiers tried to shoot me, can you imagine? I think this whole town has gone mad."

"They weren't dressed like soldiers. They were real soldiers. The town is overrun with them. They're here to take care of that zombie problem you're all facing."

"Zombie problem? You mean..."

"Hampton Cove is on lockdown, and they've been carting people off to some camp, and shooting zombies with tranq guns."

"Huh," said Vesta, wondering if that was what they'd tried to shoot her with. "I don't look like a zombie, do I?" she asked now, picking a stray banana peel from her hair.

"Yeah, you do, a bit," said Clarice, "but then to me all humans look like zombies, and all zombies look like humans. You all look pretty much the same as far as I'm concerned."

"Well, this is a fine mess I find myself in," Vesta grumbled. "So the town is locked down, and all of my family, friends and neighbors picked up. Where does that leave me?"

"To be shot down as a zombie," Clarice said. "Want a fishbone?"

"No, thanks. I have plenty of food at home, thank you very much."

"Where are your cats?"

"Oh, they're at some place called the Peppard Pet Food

Company. Odelia took them there this morning so they're quite safe."

"No, they're not," said Clarice with a chortle. "That place is like a deathtrap for pets. They do all kinds of weird experiments. You'll be glad if they make it out of there alive."

"What do you mean, weird experiments?" she asked.

"Plenty of cats have passed through that place, and the stories aren't pretty. They are subjected to all kinds of tests, act as guinea pigs for the Peppard Pet Food Company, and if they survive, their humans get free kibble for life, which isn't a big gift, as their kibble tastes horrible."

"But… why didn't you tell Max and the others!"

"Nobody asked me!"

"Oh, crap. We better get them out of there before they get hurt."

"No way, Granny. That place is like Fort Knox. No way in or out."

"We'll see about that," said Vesta, a resolute look stealing over her face. She got up and started walking off. "Well? Are you coming or not?"

Clarice hesitated for a moment. "Oh, what the hell," she finally said, and tripped after the septuagenarian.

❦

So I'd gone down the rabbit hole and I can safely say I came out the other side unscathed. Of course there was no rabbit to be found: the moment I entered the hole, the rabbit disappeared. On the other side another room awaited me, this one even nicer than the one before, with pictures of pets adorning the walls, and pet toys spread around. It started to resemble the room we'd entered when arriving in this so-called pet paradise.

"Well done!" a voice spoke over the intercom. I recognized it as Fred Peppard's. "As a reward you can eat your fill of our very special Miracle Cure Paté Delight." And to show us he meant what he said, a hatch opened in the wall and a tray emerged carrying two cans filled to the rim with paté.

Brutus and I shared a look, then shrugged.

"I guess it can't hurt to have a bite," he said.

So we approached the paté, but even before we got there the tray suddenly slid into the wall again, and the hatch closed.

"What a dirty trick!" Brutus cried.

A set of lights had switched on above the hatch. They flickered at constant intervals. Soon I discovered there was a logic to the intervals, and so before a light switched on, I put my paw on it.

"What are you doing?" asked Brutus.

"Don't you see? This place is one big test lab. They're testing us all the time, and either rewarding us or punishing us. Now you do the same, and the food will reappear."

"Oh, fine," said Brutus. "Just tell me when."

I studied the sequence, then said, "Now!" and Brutus put his paw on the light just before it flashed on.

"Excellent!" said the voice of Fred Peppard. "Now you can have your reward."

And the paté reappeared, this time sticking around long enough for us to enjoy a good helping. It tasted pretty good. Not the best paté I'd ever had, but not bad either.

"I think they're saving the really good stuff for later," I said.

Behind us, a siren blared, and Harriet and Dooley came walking through their respective holes. "It was mice this time," said Harriet.

"Mice and butterflies," said Dooley happily. "I wanted to go after the butterflies but Harriet said we should probably choose the mice instead."

"Prejudices," said Brutus. "This Fred Peppard guy is full of cat prejudices."

Dooley and Harriet proceeded to play the flashing lights game, and were rewarded with paté, just like Brutus and me.

And just when we thought that maybe this was it, and they'd finally let us go now, another hatch slid open and another toy mouse appeared.

"I think the idea is to follow the mouse," I said.

"What did I tell you?" said Brutus. "Prejudices. As if all cats like to chase mice."

"I like to chase mice," said Dooley. "I just don't like to catch them."

"I don't like mice," said Harriet. "Mice are nasty."

"Let's just do what the man expects," I said.

And so we followed the mouse into the mouse hole.

I just hoped there wouldn't be a mousetrap on the other side.

---

*O*delia and Chase walked up to the camp commander, who stood bent over a folding table, studying a map. They'd asked one of the soldiers to be taken to his commander, a colonel named Brett Spear, as they had important information on the zombies to share, and the soldier had complied.

"Yes?" Colonel Spear said without looking up. He was a large man with a perpetual scowl, a fleshy face and short bristly hair. "You have information about the creatures?"

"Yeah, first off, they're not creatures," said Odelia. "They're simply humans suffering from some kind of disease. And if you can locate my father and ask him, I'm sure he'll be able to tell you a whole lot more."

"Your father is…"

"Tex Poole. Doctor Tex Poole. He was at the hospital before, where we brought one of these so-called zombies, but he's gone missing since, and he's not at the camp either."

She was frankly worried about her dad, and also about her grandmother and uncle, who'd all gone missing and hadn't shown up at the camp so far.

"I'm Chase Kingsley," said Chase. "Chief of police. I would like to know what's going on here."

"Chief Kingsley, of course," said the colonel, for the first time showing a modicum of civility. "Well, the moment we got the call we locked down the town, and started picking up civilians for quarantining purposes. We also picked up all the zombies we could find, and have them in a separate facility, being examined as we speak. As far as we can tell they've all been affected by some type of zombie virus, and until we know how fast the virus spreads, we're going to keep your town on lockdown."

"Are you sure this is a zombie virus we're talking about?" asked Chase.

"Oh, yes," said the military commander. "Just look at them. They're zombies for sure. Now if you'll excuse me…" He resumed his study of the map. Odelia saw it was a map of Hampton Cove and surrounding towns, and she assumed soon Happy Bays and Hampton Keys would be on lockdown, too, and then maybe the entire island of Long Island!

"Do you have any idea where my father could be?" she asked now. "He's gone missing, and so have my grandmother and my uncle."

"If they're not here at the camp, they've managed to escape Hampton Cove before it was locked down," said Colonel Spear. "Let's hope they're not carrying the disease, otherwise they'll face some serious consequences." And with these words of warning, the interview was over.

They were led out again by two soldiers, and Chase dragged a hand through his hair. "Do you think your dad, Vesta and Alec managed to get out of town?"

"No, I think they're still here."

"Don't worry," said Chase, placing a comforting hand on her shoulder. "Sooner or later they'll be picked up and brought here."

34

_____

"When this is all over that Pulitzer is ours," said Jonah. "No doubt about it."

"I very much doubt that," said Libby. "Besides, we need to survive this thing first."

"Oh, we're fine," said Jonah. "Plenty of food and supplies, and the longer this lasts, the more attention we will get. Do you realize we're the only reporters inside the quarantined zone? This is our chance, Libby! Our big break! After this, we'll have our pick of assignments. Just like that reporter from *Die Hard*. That Richard Thornburg."

"You do realize that Dick Thornburg wasn't exactly the most favorite character in the movie, right? He got his lights punched out by Holly Gennero for a reason. Twice!"

Libby and Jonah had managed, through some twist of fate, to stay out of the hands of the military when they were rounding up all of Hampton Cove's citizens. They'd seen the takeover as it was happening, and had even managed to film big chunks of it, safely hidden in the bushes near Town Square. They'd seen how the zombies were shot and dragged off, and had gasped in shock, just like America would gasp in shock when they saw the images. All they needed to do now was smuggle that same shocking footage out of the town somehow. The military had, unfortunately, cut off all communications: no internet, no cell phones, no nothing. Lucky for them they had a key to the Poole place, and had been able to get at their stash of food and could even sleep in their own bed that night, while the citizenry slept in bunk beds in the makeshift military encampment.

"How long is this going to take, you think?" asked Libby as she handed the camera back to her colleague. They were staking out the camp now, and had even seen glimpses of their hostess Odelia Poole, and her mother Marge, behind the barbed-wire fence.

"Could be weeks or months," said Jonah. "Who knows? Unless all of these people suddenly start turning into zombies, too, in which case they'll go for a mass termination."

Libby gulped. "You mean…"

"Yeah, mass killings, mass graves. And we'll be right here filming the whole thing."

"I'm not sure I even want to be here when that happens," she said. She liked the Pooles, and had enjoyed their hospitality and their friendship. She even felt for them, what with their peculiar grandmother and her fertility obsession. And now this.

"We're not here to judge, Libby," said Jonah as he shoved a piece of gum into his mouth. "We're simply here to observe and report. The eyes of the world will soon be on this town, unless they catch us, too. If that happens, no one will ever know, and the military will be able to carry out their plans with absolute impunity."

"They've got to do something, Jonah. If this zombie epidemic continues to spread, it might take over the entire island, then the state, and then the country!"

"Oh, they'll contain it, have no fear. They have experience with this sort of thing."

"How do you know so much about all this zombie stuff?"

"Because I watch YouTube, silly!" he said. "And you should, too."

Jonah was a conspiracy buff, and liked all those weird conspiracy websites where everything that happened, from the big news stories to the mundane, was turned into a conspiracy. Frankly Libby found the whole thing a little tiring, and had always wondered how Jonah could stand to watch that nonsense. But now, with this zombie thing happening, she had to admit that maybe there was some truth to his crazy theories.

"Too bad we can't get any reception," she said as she checked her phone again. "Otherwise we could transmit the footage now, and tell Lionel what's going on."

Lionel Noonan was their editor, and would be over the moon when he heard what they'd stumbled into down here.

"Let's go back to the house," said Jonah. "Nothing is happening and I'm starving."

Careful to stay out of sight, they retreated from their position and started making their way back to town. They had to be careful and avoid military patrols, but apart from that it was all very exciting, Libby had to admit. Except for the constant fear that she, too, would turn into a zombie. But if that happened, Jonah had promised her, he'd make sure he got the whole transition on tape. And then bash her head in in a mercy killing.

A very comforting thought indeed.

They arrived back at the Poole house and snuck inside. It was weird walking down streets that were completely deserted, and past houses whose front doors were still open and where toys littered the front lawns. On the streets, children's bikes lay immobile, and cars haphazardly sat parked in the middle of the road. Almost as if its occupants had all suddenly been beamed up, or disintegrated.

One moment the town had been teeming with life, and the next... nothing.

She walked up to the fridge when she saw a note stuck to it with a pineapple magnet.

'Going to check out Peppard Pet Food Company. Suspicious activity reported by Clarice. Gran. PS: no one touch my hormone shake (the green bottle). I mean it!'

Libby smiled and saw that, indeed, a green bottle was in the fridge. In fact an entire collection of green bottles, and they all had a warning written on them: 'Do Not Touch! I'm not kidding!'

Yep. Grandma Muffin was not a lady to be trifled with. She took out a bottle of orange juice and took a sip, then wondered how Vesta had managed to escape capture by the military. And what she meant by suspicious activity at the Peppard Pet Food Company.

She vaguely remembered Odelia telling her something about her pets wrangling an invitation to enter some kind of testing program at Peppard's, and now this.

"Jonah?" she said when her partner in crime ambled into the kitchen. "Look at this."

Jonah read the note, and shrugged. "So?"

"Why would Vesta find it necessary to go to this Peppard place now, with this zombie thing happening? And who is Clarice?"

"Probably a friend of hers. Who cares? Vesta is obviously a nutcase."

"I think she's actually pretty clever. Eccentric, sure, but not a nut."

Jonah was peering into the fridge and not liking what he saw.

"Wanna go over there and check it out?"

"No, I definitely don't want to visit a pet food company, Libby. What's the news value?"

"I'm not sure, but I've got this hunch."

"You and your hunches. Remember you had a hunch Bill Gates was actually a woman named Jill?"

"Okay, fine. I dropped the ball on that one. But this time I'm sure there's something there. Vesta wouldn't go off on a wild-goose chase. She's much too smart for that. I'm sure this is connected to the zombie thing."

"And I'm hungry and I don't want to risk going outside and running into a military patrol and getting locked up in that camp. Pretty sure the food is terrible in there."

"Fine," she said. "Then I'll go by myself."

He looked up. "Are you nuts? You can't go by yourself. What if you get caught? Then I'll be all alone out here, without my reporter. You know I can't ad-lib, Libby."

"So come with me. If it turns out to be nothing, no harm done. Besides, Vesta is still the main topic of our documentary, and we shouldn't leave her side no matter what."

"Yeah, as if that documentary will ever see the light of day."

She made for the door. "See you later," she said. "Don't wait up."

"Hey, wait!"

And then he was trailing after her. She smiled. "Can't miss me, can you, pardner?"

"How am I going to win my Pulitzer without my trusty reporter?"

She rolled her eyes. "You're a real prince, aren't you, Jonah Zappa?"

"And don't I know it."

And then they were off, for another long trek through Hampton Cove. If nothing else, she would have lost at least five pounds by the time this assignment was finally over.

35

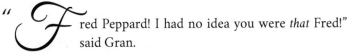

"Fred Peppard! I had no idea you were *that* Fred!" said Gran.

"Vesta Muffin. Long time no see!"

As we watched the reacquaintance taking place, I was actually relieved that Gran knew Mr. Peppard. Maybe she could talk some sense into him and make him set us free. I mean, it's all well and good to play games all day, and be rewarded with some fine pet food, but at some point a cat just wants to be home and take a nap on his favorite couch.

"And look how old you've gotten!" said Gran.

"Not you, Vesta," said Mr. Peppard. "You haven't changed a bit."

"Still the charmer, aren't you, Fred?"

"Only when in the company of a beautiful woman like yourself. So what brings you here?"

"These are my cats," she said, gesturing to the four of us. "So I figured I better check and see if you haven't been mistreating them."

"Oh, I would never hurt a pet, you know that. All I do is

put them through our test program and give them some of the finest pet food as a reward."

"Mh. Last time I saw you, you were selling life insurance door to door."

"Yeah, well, last time we met you were still married to that crook what's-his-name..."

She held up a hand. "Let's not talk about he-who-should-not-be-named—may he rest in peace."

"Oh, Jack died, did he?"

"Yeah, and good riddance, too. Can you believe he had the gall to cheat on me with my best friend—ex-friend now, of course?"

"Yeah, actually I can. Jack always was something of a scoundrel."

"So were you, if I remember correctly."

He laughed. "Oh, Vesta. Your tongue is still as sharp as ever."

"Gran, ask him about Zebediah Clam," I said. "He was in here just before you arrived, discussing something with Mr. Peppard."

"Yeah, and he was very angry with Mr. Peppard, too," said Dooley. "Calling him all kinds of names."

"And while you're at it, maybe you can tell him that the way he treats his guests stinks," said Brutus.

"Yeah, locking us up in cages and making us jump through hoops all day long," said Harriet. "I don't like it here, Gran. This place sucks. He makes us work for our food!"

Gran, who'd listened but couldn't reply, merely gave us an imperceptible nod. Her eyes glittered when she said, "I heard you and Zebediah Clam are pretty close? He's my doctor, you see."

Fred Peppard's eyebrows shot up. "Your doctor. Is that a fact?"

"Yeah, he's helping me get pregnant again. Fertility treatment." Fred burst into raucous laughter, earning himself a dark scowl from Gran. "Oh, and that's funny to you, is it? Well, thank you very much, Fred."

"No, I'm sorry, Vesta," he said, wiping away tears of laughter. "It's just…" He laughed again. "Zeb told me he was working a client in town. If I'd known it was you, I would have told him to back away slowly and run for the hills."

"What the hell are you talking about?" she asked, hands on hips now, eyes blazing.

"Zeb isn't a fertility expert. He's been conning you, Vesta, my dear. He probably knows just about as much about fertility treatments as me, and I'm just a salesman, as you pointed out."

"He's not a fertility expert? But I found his name in the medical file of this ex-friend I mentioned. This woman is my age and still on the pill."

"All bogus," said Fred decidedly. "Zeb may be a lot of things, but he's no doctor."

"But I saw his degree. It's on his website."

"Probably made it himself in Photoshop."

"But his site is full of testimonials."

"Must have written them himself."

She was staring at the man, her voice having taken on a belligerent tone. "Then why the hell are you even involved with him, Fred?"

Fred shrugged. "He's a businessman, same as me. He sees an opportunity to make some money, he grabs it, milks it for all it's worth, then moves on."

"I don't believe this. He's been feeding me hormone cocktails."

"Probably sugar water. How much are you paying him?"

"Five grand, and another ten for the IVF."

"Don't let him fool you, Vesta. And I'm telling you this as

a friend. The man is a crook, and he'll simply take your money and skedaddle."

She looked disappointed now. "But... he promised me I'd be the world's oldest mom."

"Yeah, well, what can I tell you? You've been swindled, and if it makes you feel any better, you're not the first one either. I'm sure plenty of women fell for the guy's hustle."

"That rotten, no-good scoundrel!" she cried, shaking her fist. "If I get my hands on him!"

"Don't tell him I told you," said Fred. "I still have to work with the guy. We're business partners."

"You're working with this damn crook?"

"The man talks a good game. He can probably sell eggs to a chicken."

"He's a louse, a maggot, a rat, a skunk, a dirtbag, a fungus and a douche," she snapped. "I'm taking my cats, Fred. They're needed elsewhere."

"Oh, sure. I was actually trying to get in touch with you—though the contact person was listed as one Odelia Poole?"

"My granddaughter."

"So Marge had a daughter, huh?"

"Yeah, she married a doctor."

"Doctor? Nice. Listen, your cats are pretty special. Real smart. So I'd like to run some more tests and—"

"Sorry, Fred. No can do," said Gran. Obviously Fred's association with the louse, maggot, rat, skunk, dirtbag, fungus and douche Zebediah Clam didn't sit well with her.

"But..."

"Come on, you guys," said Gran. "Let's get you out of here."

"Well, it was sure nice to see you again, Vesta."

"Likewise," she said, but didn't sound happy.

"Listen, try to steer clear of those darn roadblocks, you

hear? The army seems to be all over the place all of a sudden. Good thing I'm right outside the town limits."

"Yeah, I found a way around the roadblocks," she said, giving Clarice a pointed look.

"That's great. Oh, and please don't tell Zeb I spilled the beans, will you?"

"I won't," said Gran. "But I can't promise you will get your business partner back in one piece. In fact when I lay my hands on the son of a monkey it won't be his lucky day."

*O*nce we were outside, Gran crouched down with some effort, then said, "And now tell me everything you know about our dear Doctor Clam."

So we told Gran the whole story, from the moment we arrived at the clinic, and were locked up in metal cages, to the conversation we overheard between Fred and Clam. Her lips formed a thin line.

"I'm going to get that bastard," she said. "I'm going to get him and make him drink his filthy hormone cocktails. Or better yet, I'll give him an enema with his own concoction."

"They're clearly working together, Gran," I said. "And it's got something to do with the zombies, too."

"Yeah, well. That wouldn't surprise me," she said. "Clam is a crook, and Fred is an even bigger crook. I have no idea what's going on here, but I'm going to find out. But first we need to get back to the house without being arrested, shot, or killed. So if you sniff out a military patrol, you tell me, all right?"

And then we were on our way back to town.

"So how did you find us, Clarice?" asked Dooley.

"Oh, easy," said Clarice. "I've heard so many horror stories about this Peppard Pet Food place over the years that I decided to give your gran a helping paw."

"You knew about this place and you didn't tell us?" said Harriet,

"You never asked, all right? Besides, when something looks too good to be true, like free kibble for life? It's because it probably is."

"Yeah, we learned our lesson," said Dooley. "Fred Peppard is not a nice man. And his pet food paradise isn't a pet food paradise at all."

"At least you got out of there with your health and your sanity," she said. "I once knew a cat who was never the same again after passing through Peppard's program. She couldn't stop chasing fictitious rabbits down fictitious rabbit holes and kept seeing flashing lights she had to put out. Sad."

We'd climbed an incline and Gran glanced in the direction of town.

"We need to watch our backs from here on out," she announced.

"Maybe we should move in the other direction?" I said. "Go to Happy Bays instead and warn people about what's going on here?"

"I'm not leaving my family behind, Max," said Gran. "No way. And I'm not going to be scared off by a couple of so-called zombies and a couple of idiots dressed up as soldiers."

"Who's that?" asked Brutus suddenly.

We all looked in the direction he was pointing.

It was a zombie, and he was coming our way!

36

In the camp, dinner was served. It was a sober affair, and not exactly a feast. In fact the only thing on the menu was some kind of slop that could have been meat, more slop that could have been potatoes, and a third kind of slop that probably were vegetables.

They were seated at long wooden tables inside a khaki-colored tent, and the atmosphere was downcast. Odelia and her mom and Chase were seated together, but she couldn't stop worrying about her dad, her uncle, her grandmother, and her cats.

"How long is this going to take?" asked Marge. "How long before we can go home?"

"No idea, Marge," said Chase.

"I wonder what happened to Gran," said Odelia. "And Dad. And Uncle Alec. Is it possible there's more than one camp? That they were taken to another one?"

"I don't think so," said Chase. "As far as I can tell the other camp is for the zombies, and they're probably treated a little differently than we are."

"You mean their food is worse than ours?" said Marge. "I find that hard to believe."

They ate in silence, as did most people. Suddenly a woman started screaming, "Zombies! It's the zombies! They're attacking us!"

But as they looked around, there was no sign of any zombies anywhere.

"People are losing it," said Marge. "They're seeing zombies everywhere."

"I don't get it, though," said Odelia. "If these really were zombies, wouldn't they have made more casualties? As far as I can tell these are pretty peaceful zombies, only interested in attacking bodies of water, not actual human bodies."

"Yeah, if they're zombies, they're the weirdest zombies I ever heard of," Chase agreed.

"I just hope Alec is all right," said Marge, "and your grand-mother. And Tex."

The worst part about being confined inside a camp like this, without a phone and any other means of communication, was the lack of information. They had no idea what was going on outside, and no way of knowing what had happened to their loved ones.

Dan Goory approached and bent down to whisper in her ear, "I hope you're taking notes. When this is all over I'm putting out a monster edition of the *Gazette*. Pun intended."

"If this will ever be over," she said.

"Oh, now don't you go all Debbie Downer on me, honey," he said with a smile. "Of course this will be over at some point. They'll simply get rid of all the zombies and soon life will be back to normal. With a monster circulation of the *Gazette* as a consequence."

He patted her on the back and was off to get a second helping of the triple slop.

"At least someone is looking at the bright side of this mess," said Chase.

"Dan is a newspaperman. And a newspaperman recognizes a chance to make headlines when he sees it," said Marge. "Speaking of which, what happened to Libby and Jonah?"

Odelia had to admit she'd completely forgotten about Doctor Clam's television crew. "And what happened to Doctor Clam?" she said. "I haven't seen him around either."

Lots of questions, and no answers. For a reporter it was not a fun time!

Then again, maybe Dan was right, and she should start taking notes. She could interview people at the camp, and start working on a series of articles about the day the zombie apocalypse touched down in her town.

At least it would take her mind off things.

&

"Get behind me, you guys," said Vesta. "I'll give this zombie a poke in the snoot if he comes any closer."

She'd picked up a tree branch and was ready to hammer the zombie until he thought better than to attack an innocent and sweet old lady out for a walk with her five cats.

"Excuse me!" said the zombie. "Um, can you please tell me where I am?"

It was the first time Vesta had ever heard of zombies actually talking, but she wasn't going to let a minor detail like that diminish her vigilance.

"Not one step closer!" she yelled. "I'm warning you! I have a weapon and I'm not afraid to use it!"

The zombie hesitated. He looked just like all the other zombies she'd seen on the television: really bad skin and a staggering gait. Though he did look a little more intelligent than his brain-devouring buddies. In fact it wasn't too much to say that he looked keen to make her acquaintance. "Um, I'm sorry," he said, halting in his tracks. "I seem to have gotten lost somehow. So if you could please point me in the direction of the nearest town, I could call my wife and ask her to come pick me up. Or if I could borrow your phone for a second? I seem to have misplaced mine."

"Your wife? What are you talking about?"

This was the first she'd heard of a zombie asking to call his wife. Then again, even zombies had wives and husbands, presumably. Zombie wives and zombie husbands.

"Well, I seem to find myself in something of a pickle," the zombie explained. "I remember being dropped off at the clinic, but then I seem to have lost a chunk of time until I woke up just now, feeling a little disoriented, and frankly a little dizzy, too. I don't think I've eaten for a while." He took another step closer.

"Oh, no!" she said, heaving that tree branch higher. "You're not coming anywhere near my brains, you zombie!"

"Brains?" He laughed. "Oh, but I'm not interested in your brains, ma'am. In fact I don't think I've ever eaten brains in my life." He shivered. "I don't think I'd like it. But I could go for a nice burger, or even a slice of pizza and a mega-sized Coke to wash it all down."

She lowered the branch. This was some weird-ass zombie.

"Be careful, Gran," said Harriet. "It's probably just a trick to make you lower your guard. The moment you drop that stick he'll pounce on you and scoop out your brains!"

Gran raised her makeshift weapon. "Do you have a name?" she asked, starting to think this dude might not be as zombieish as the rest of them.

"Ned," he said. "Ned Gorecki from Milwaukee. If I could

179

just call my wife Marla and ask her to come pick me up, I'd be much obliged. Pretty sure she's worried sick by now."

"I don't get it. If you're from Milwaukee, what the hell are you doing on Long Island?"

"I'm still on Long Island? That's good to know. Well, a friend of mine tipped me off about becoming a medical volunteer. Said there was this clinic looking for volunteers and they were offering eight thousand dollars a week. And since the Gorecki family bank account is in a bad way right now, I figured I might as well give it a shot. So I applied and was immediately accepted into the program, which started on a Monday." He frowned. "What day is today, by the way? I seem to have lost track of time completely."

"Friday," said Gran.

"Oh, my. That means I lost an entire week. How peculiar."

Gran was starting to get an idea of what was going on here. "You don't happen to remember the name of this clinic, do you?"

"Oh, yes, of course. Um, ClamPep Laboratories. They run these programs all the time, mainly for the big pharmaceutical companies, but for smaller players, too. This one was for a company called Zephyr Industries. Pharmaceutical solutions. But like I said, I seem to have lost an entire week since the program began, but I suppose it must have ended, for I woke up at the foot of this little hill, with no recollection of the last couple of days."

"Are you by any chance very, very thirsty?" she asked.

"Oh, I'm parched," said Ned. "Absolutely parched. In fact the first thought that passed through my mind when I woke up just now was where to find something to drink."

"The ocean is that way," said Gran, pointing in the direction of Hampton Cove.

"Oh, thank you so much!" he said. "Maybe I'll make my

way over there and dunk my head in the water. All I seem to be able to think about is plunging in and soaking it up."

"Ocean water is briny, though," said Max. "He won't be rehydrated if he jumps into the ocean."

"No, he won't," said Gran, "but he doesn't mind. All he wants is water—any water."

"Um, who are you talking to?" asked Ned.

"No one. Listen, buddy. That's a fascinating story you just told me, and it sure answers a lot of questions about what's been happening in my town lately. Would you mind accompanying me into the next town and telling the same story you just told me to the police over there? I'm sure they'd be very interested in what you have to say."

"The police? But why?"

"Because I think you were bamboozled, same way I was bamboozled by this ClamPep Laboratories of yours, and the same way my cats were bamboozled."

"What's bamboozled, Max?" asked Dooley.

"Cheated," said Max.

"I think mistreated is a better word," said Harriet.

"Screwed over, I'd say," said Clarice.

"Yeah, royally screwed," Brutus grumbled.

"So the zombies... aren't really zombies at all?" asked Dooley.

"No, they're just people," said Max, "and victims of some medical experiment."

"Oh, dear," said Dooley. "That's not very nice."

Just then, two more people appeared on the horizon. They weren't military, Gran saw, but her television crew. She waved them over, and when they'd joined her, Jonah huffing and puffing and Libby's cheeks red from the exertion of the long hike, she said, "I want you to interview this gentleman and get his story on tape, okay? And then we're all going to the police in Happy Bays to file a complaint against Fred Peppard and Zebediah Clam."

"A zombie!" said Jonah. "Cool!"

"Excuse me, ma'am," said Ned. "Why does everyone keep calling me a zombie?"

Gran handed him a little pocket mirror and the man took one look at his face, squealed something fierce then dropped it.

"I'm a zombie!" he said. "What did they do to me!"

"Oh, bummer," said Jonah. "He's not a real zombie, is he?"

"No, he's just a dude from Milwaukee," said Gran, "who's been royally screwed over," she added with a wink to her cats.

So Jonah pointed his camera at Ned Gorecki, Libby cleared her throat, and then the poor guy repeated his story for the camera, the building of Fred Peppard's Pet Food Company in the background. Or, as it was apparently also known, ClamPep Labs.

*L*ibby and Jonah had finished their interview with Ned Gorecki, who kept smacking his lips until Libby had the good sense to offer him her water bottle. He drained it in one glug-glugging motion, then, when Jonah offered him his, poured it out over his head.

Yep, the man was parched, all right.

We started on our long trek into the next town, and when a car passed and pulled over, Gran quickly made her way over, hoping to catch a ride.

Suddenly, before our very eyes, she went berserk! She started screaming at the man, then tried to drag him out of the car and slapped his face repeatedly, while he fended her off until he managed to slam his door and was gone, tires spinning and kicking up dust.

"Come back here, you scum!"

And as he passed us, I saw that the driver was none other than… Doctor Clam!

"I don't think Gran will become the oldest mother in the world, will she, Max?" asked Dooley.

"Doubtful," I agreed. "She might become the oldest woman in the world to kick a con man's ass, though."

"Hey, that was Doctor Clam!" said Ned suddenly as he stared after the car, which wasn't going to Hampton Cove, but the other direction instead. Doctor Zebediah Clam was probably feeling the heat his medical experiments had wrought.

"You know that guy?" asked Libby.

"Oh, sure. He's the doctor in charge of the medical side of the program. He measures out the dosages and decides which drugs we all have to take. He's a real medical genius."

"Yeah, a real genius," Jonah echoed acerbically, then hoisted his camera back on his shoulder and pointed it at the hapless zombie. "Please comment on Doctor Zebediah Clam, Mr. Gorecki. How would you describe him and his role in the medical program?"

And then he and Libby were off for a short addendum to their original interview.

We took the road that leads from Hampton Cove to Happy Bays, our neighboring town. It wasn't a long trek, all things considered, and when we finally arrived in town, people all stared at the strange procession of an old lady, two reporters, a zombie, and five cats. Clarice had decided to tag along, seeing as her schedule was clear, and she had a vested interest in ridding our town of the zombies, since a town without people is also a town without food being dumped in dumpsters, her preferred source of nourishment.

We arrived at the Happy Bays police station, and walked in. A nice lady with pretty cornrows greeted us cordially, and escorted us to an interview room after listening to Gran's harangue.

Moments later, a gangly police officer arrived, sporting a prominent and very mobile Adam's apple, and introduced himself as officer Virgil Scattering.

184

He cleared his throat noisily, stared at the zombie for a moment, then took out pad and pencil and sat poised for further developments. "So you, sir, are a zombie?" he asked.

"Not a zombie," Gran corrected him. "Ned here has been duped by a malicious lab run by a fake doctor who turned him into a zombie and set him loose on the streets of my town, which is now on lockdown because of this so-called zombie invasion."

The officer gulped. "So… you admit that you are, in fact, a zombie, sir?" he asked.

"No, I'm not a zombie," said Ned. "Though I am very thirsty. Could I have some—"

"Brains?" asked Officer Scattering nervously. "No, you can't. I still need them."

He didn't look like he had a lot of brains to dispense with, but when it was finally established that Ned just needed water, the officer obliged and got him some, which Ned sucked up like a sponge. The man could probably drink his body weight in water.

"So when did you first decide you wanted to become a zombie?" the officer asked.

"Look, I'm not a zombie, all right?" said Ned, starting to get a little annoyed.

"But you look like a zombie," Officer Scattering pointed out, aptly drawing a doodle on his notepad of a zombie having his head bashed in with a big baseball bat.

"I may look like a zombie, but that doesn't make me one, all right?" said Ned, quite correctly, I thought.

"We have a strict rule about zombies in this town," said Officer Scattering. "And the rule is that we don't allow them. Zombies create more zombies, and before you know it the whole town is overrun with them, and then the military come in and the whole thing becomes a mess. So I would simply advise you to go home, which presumably is the graveyard you were buried in when you died, and please don't come back here."

"But I'm not dead!"

"You look dead to me, sir."

"I'm telling you, I'm not a zombie! I'm the victim of a malicious medical experiment!"

"Well, that I can believe. Nevertheless. You died, then decided for some reason to return from the dead, and now I have to advise you to return to the safety of your coffin."

"But—"

"Leave life to the living, Mr. Zombie. And return to your dead."

"But I—"

"Much simpler that way. Cleaner, if you see what I mean."

"But I'm not a zombie!"

"A living dead person, then. Or an undead person? A walking dead?"

"My name is Ned Gorecki."

"Oh, so you have a name!" said the officer, jotting this down in his notes.

"Of course I have a name! Just like you have a name, and this gentleman with the camera over here has a name, and the old lady over there—just like we all have names!"

Ned was getting a little worked up, I could tell, and no wonder. The cop wasn't making things easy for him.

"The thing is, sir," said Officer Scattering, clearing his throat noisily, "and I'm going to be absolutely frank with you here. Put all my cards on the table. I'm not an expert on zombies. I don't even watch your show, to be honest. Too gruesome for my taste. But by all means, I salute you on your success. People love your show, and good for you."

"Look, can you just take his statement?" said Gran. "Without all the gibberish about zombies? Ned wants to file a complaint against Fred Peppard and Zebediah Clam of ClamPep Laboratories. And while you're at it, you better talk to my son over in Hampton Cove, and tell him—"

"Is your son a zombie, too?"

"No, he's not," said Gran, gritting her teeth a little.

Officer Scattering returned his attention to Ned. "Did you bring any of your zombie friends? Because I have to tell you that Chief Whitehouse is not going to be happy about this visit. Like I said, we have a strict no-zombie policy in this town. Very strict."

"Look, isn't there someone else we can talk to? This Chief Whitehouse, maybe?"

Officer Scattering smiled a deprecating little smile. "Oh, no. No, no, no. The Chief doesn't deal with minor matters like this. The Chief only deals with murders and such. Now if your zombie had murdered someone—have you murdered someone, Mr. Zombie?"

"This is insane," said Ned, shaking his head.

"I agree," said the officer. "Which is why I never watch your show. Too much crazy."

The door opened and a large man with a jowly face, a deep scowl and a bristly buzzcut stuck his head in. "What's all this nonsense about zombies?" He took one look at Ned and his frown deepened. "We don't condone zombies in Happy Bays, sir. So I suggest you go right back to where you came from and be real quick about it, too."

"I am not a zombie!"

"Yeah, yeah. That's what they all say."

Lucky for us Gran didn't lose her cool. In a few short words she explained to this Chief Whitehouse what was going on in Hampton Cove, and to his credit the man finally grasped the urgency of the situation and got on the phone with the proper authorities.

We were all transferred to his office, much to the disappointment of Officer Scattering, who seemed to have enjoyed his interview with a zombie, and as we watched, Chief Whitehouse talked to the County Executive, then the Governor, and finally some colonel called Brett Spear.

Finally, when he hung up and placed two large hands on his desk, he said, "I think I've got it all straightened out. This colonel said the zombies are starting to wake up, and some of them have come to their senses, just like Mr. Ned Gorecki here. He'll have your Fred Peppard picked up, and your Zebediah Clam, and take a good hard look at ClamPep Laboratories. I want to thank you, Mrs. Muffin, for bringing this matter to my attention."

"My son speaks very highly of you, Chief Whitehouse," she said. "And now I can see why. You are a credit to your community and a man after my own heart."

Rare praise from the lips of a person as crusty as Gran, I thought. But she was right.

"Chief Alec and I have been friends for many years," said the Chief, leaning back, "and I can honestly say this is the first time one of his cases has spilled over into my town. Yes, Virgil, what do you want!" he boomed when Officer Scattering's face popped up in the Chief's office door window for the third time in the space of under a minute.

Virgil opened the door and handed the Chief a baseball bat.

"What the hell is this?" asked the Chief.

"A baseball bat, sir. In case you want to take care of the zombie. A good quick hit on the top of the head should do the trick." He smiled. "I looked it up on the internet. Bashing a zombie's brains in seems to be the best way to deal with them. Sad but true."

"I don't believe this," said the Chief, shaking his head.

"It's all in the wrist, sir," said Virgil, demonstrating his skill.

"I'm not a zombie!" Ned screamed.

"Of course not, Mr. Zombie. Of course not."

I had a feeling it wouldn't be the last time someone mistook Ned for a zombie. At least until he got rid of that extreme rash.

EPILOGUE

*I*t was barbecue time at the Pooles, and Tex was manning his grill like nobody's business, distributing patties and sausages left, right and center. In fact there was no human, animal or zombie who didn't get a piece of meat from the grill maestro.

Life in Hampton Cove had finally returned to normal, the camp had been closed down, the curfew and quarantine measures lifted, and the tanks rolled back to their military barracks where they would remain until the next zombie invasion broke out.

Doctor Zebediah Clam and Fred Peppard had been arrested, and the remaining patients of their ClamPep Labs released. Turns out they offered their services not just to companies wanting to test their dodgy products on humans, but on pets, too, and we'd been lucky that on the day we were admitted to their testing facility, only an innocent behavioral study had been conducted, and not a more deleterious application.

The zombies had all recovered from their ordeal, and no longer looked like zombies at all. Ned Gorecki had returned to his wife and family in Milwaukee to what I hoped would be a long and happy life.

Harsh words had been spoken about the rash decision to put Hampton Cove on lockdown, and the report Libby and Jonah had put out had stirred up a media storm.

All in all, though, all was well that ended well, and five cats and five humans enjoyed a nice balmy day in the Poole backyard.

"I can't believe you slept through the whole thing!" said Odelia.

"Yeah, I guess being suspended has its advantages," said Uncle Alec, filling his plate with relish. "I only woke up when the tanks rumbled past my house, on their way out of town."

"Maybe it was a good thing," said Marge. "It wasn't much fun being in that camp."

"It wasn't a lot of fun being in that zombie camp," said Tex. "Especially since no one was allowed near the zombies, who were considered highly infectious and dangerous."

"A toast," said Chase, raising a bottle of beer. "To the heroine of the hour. Maybe not the oldest mother in the world, but definitely the person who saved us from the zombie apocalypse. Vesta Muffin!"

"Oh, you guys," said Vesta as glasses were raised in her honor. "It was all a big coincidence, really. If I hadn't been chased by those soldiers who thought I was a zombie and who tried to shoot me, I'd never have hidden in that dumpster and met Clarice, and she would never have shown me the way to Fred Peppard's place."

"You saved the day, Gran," said Odelia. "And I think that calls for a celebration." She planted a big kiss on her grandmother's cheek, and it was obvious the old lady was pleased as punch.

"The best thing happened this morning," said Gran. "When I ran into Scarlett Canyon at Rory Suds's pharmacy, and I told her that her doctor is a quack and now in jail. You should have seen her face! Turns out Clam had been selling her fertility shots and she'd been injecting herself for months now, believing his lies, same way I did."

"Injecting herself with what?" asked Marge.

"Snake oil, probably," said Chase.

"Rory had one of her dosages tested—turns out he gave her an innocent saline solution. Costs cents on the dollar and he sold it to her for three thousand a pop."

"That man has no shame," said Marge, shaking her head.

"So do zombies exist or not?" asked Dooley now.

"Pretty sure they don't," I said.

"Yeah, pretty sure there are no zombies," said Brutus.

"At least one good thing has come from all of this," said Harriet. And she gestured to the bags of cat kibble piled high on a corner of the deck. It was part of a larger shipment. The entire contents of the Peppard Pet Food Company's warehouse had been distributed free of charge amongst Hampton Cove's pet owners, since it was their pets who'd suffered most at the hands of the company's owners, and so now we had pet food for life.

"I don't think it's actually for life, though," I said. "Not really. Those pellets have an expiration date, and if we don't eat them real quick they'll just end up in a dumpster."

"Which is good news for me," said Clarice. "You can say many things about Fred Peppard, but not that he doesn't know how to make some really tasty pet food."

"Yeah, at least in that respect he wasn't a charlatan," I agreed.

"But if zombies don't exist," said Dooley, still following his own train of thought, "what about vampires? Or elves or leprechauns or gnomes or goblins or gremlins?"

"All these mythical creatures don't actually exist," I said.

"Though wouldn't it be nice if they did?" said Harriet dreamily. "Life would be so much fun!"

"Who cares about fun?" Clarice grumbled. "Just give me a nice juicy rat from time to time, that's all the fun I need."

I shivered. Not exactly my idea of fun. Then again, all creatures on God's green earth are different, and that's what makes it so fascinating to be alive. This past week alone we'd met zombies and cats and dogs and hamsters and guinea pigs and even turtles, and all of them had enriched our lives in some way. Well, maybe not the zombies. They were a little gruesome to look at. Lucky for us they had proven fake zombies in the end.

Clarice wandered off in the direction of the grill, where grill master Tex could always be relied on to dispense a few patties to anyone who cared to open their mouths, and Harriet and Brutus snuck through the opening in the hedge for a nap—or nookie?

"I still think zombies exist, Max," said Dooley. "I just don't think we met the right zombies."

"And let's hope we never do, Dooley," I said. "I don't think we'd enjoy the experience."

"Maybe we would. Zombies lead a simple life: all they care about is their next meal. Like cows."

"I'd rather meet a cow in a dark alley than a zombie, though," I admitted.

Then again, the chances of meeting a cow in a dark alley were decidedly slim. But then so were the chances of meeting a zombie.

All in all I was glad this adventure was over. And just as I'd closed my eyes and was starting to fall asleep, suddenly a zombie came crashing through the bushes and alarmed us all.

"Save yourselves!" the zombie cried. "Save yourselves from the zombie apocalypse!"

Upon closer inspection, it was Father Reilly, and he didn't look well.

"Father Reilly!" Marge cried. "My God, what happened to you!"

"I was shot and locked up with a horde of raging zombies!" said the wild-eyed priest, whose clothes were tattered, his face streaked with mud. "But I managed to escape, and have been hiding out in the woods for days! Where are the zombies? Have they gone?"

"They weren't zombies," said Tex, watching on as Father Reilly grabbed a patty from the grill and shoved it into his mouth, then spat it out again.

"Hot hot hot!" the man breathed. "What do you mean, no zombies?"

"They were just given some bad drugs," said Odelia. "That gave them a terrible rash and affected their nervous system and made them lose their minds. They're fine now."

"Lies!" the priest cried. "All lies! Save yourselves while you still can!"

And he crashed into those bushes again.

"Father Reilly!" Marge cried. "Come back!"

But the priest was gone, presumably to return to his cherished woods. He reminded me of those soldiers in Vietnam who were never informed that the war was over.

"Poor man," said Odelia. "He's clearly lost it."

And so Uncle Alec and Chase set off to retrieve the confused priest.

See what I mean? A nice zombie invasion brings us all closer together. Which is a good thing, wouldn't you agree? It had gotten Uncle Alec his old job back, now that all that nasty gossip about him and Pamela Witherspoon had finally stopped, and it had even caused Gran and Scarlett Canyon to put their differences aside long enough to rail against Doc Clam, their common foe. So much to be thankful for.

"Do you think cows can be zombies, Max?" asked Dooley now.

"I doubt it, Dooley," I said.

"Okay." He paused, then: "How about chickens?"

"Um…"

"Or dogs or ducks?"

"Well, theoretically anything can be brought back to life, I guess."

He smiled. "I like that, Max. I like that very much."

"But why are you so adamant on zombies existing, Dooley?"

"Because everyone has a right to be alive, Max, even dead things. Life is so wonderful—why should we be the only ones that get to enjoy it?"

And then he put his head on his paws and dozed off, a happy smile on his face.

I watched as he slept, and thought of something Father Reilly was fond of saying: blessed are the pure of heart. For some reason Dooley always came to mind when I heard those words. And maybe my friend was right. Life was so precious even the dead deserved a taste of it. Though maybe, for the sake of my equanimity, not anytime soon!

EXCERPT FROM MURDER AT THE ART CLASS

Chapter One

"Did you see the new guy?"

Clara's voice was barely above a whisper, clearly awed to be sharing the same space with this 'new guy'.

"Yes, I've seen him," said Emily. "In fact I was the one who suggested this position."

Clara's eyes turned to her friend and colleague. "You *know* him?"

Em shrugged while she turned off the heaving and coughing coffee machine and placed two cups of espresso macchiato on a tray and added spoons and spiced gingerbread muffins with salted caramel frosting. "He's in my life drawing class."

"No way!" said Clara, a robust ginger-haired young woman. "Don't tell me this is one of those *nude* life drawing classes?"

Emily nodded, suppressing a tiny smile as she watched Clara's eyes go wide as saucers. "Yup. Buck-nekkid."

"Oh. My. God! Where is this class? I totally have to sign up!"

"I told you about my class before, remember? And you told me you didn't have a single artistic bone in your body and therefore weren't eligible."

"That was before I knew there were nekkid men prancing about."

"They don't prance about. They just... lie there."

"I'll bet there's lots and lots of women in your class," said Clara, dreamily following the new guy's every movement as he wended his way through the room, serving customers of the Roast Bean with a deft flourish.

"Lots and lots," Emily confirmed dryly. In fact this season they'd seen record attendance at the Community Arts School where she'd been a volunteer for the past two years. The school offered adult classes in dance, music, theater and drawing, apart from its daytime high school curriculum. It wasn't the school she'd attended, being a transplant from Pennsylvania, but it was the school located just around the corner from where she lived in Bushwick, Brooklyn and the school where her roommate Ansel spent his formative years.

"He's coming," said Clara in urgent tones. She pushed at her ginger curls. "How do I look?"

Emily gave her friend a once-over. "You look fine, Clara. Though I wouldn't get my hopes up. I have a feeling John's roving eye has already landed elsewhere."

Clara's own eye flicked back to the new barista and her face crumpled. "Who?!"

It didn't take her long to figure it out for herself, though. John Sunderland, the young man who'd recently joined the Roast Bean's employ, was chatting up a young waitress who'd also just joined their ranks. The young woman in question was stunning, no doubt about it, and seemed to enjoy the attention John was lavishing on her with visible relish.

"Of course," grunted Clara. "Ken would fall for Barbie's charm, wouldn't he?" She threw up her hands. "It's just not fair! Why can't us mere mortals ever catch a break?"

"I wouldn't be too disappointed if I were you," said Emily.

"What is that supposed to mean?"

"Young John Sunderland is a heartbreaker, honey."

"I see what you mean," said Clara, her gaze landing on yet another new addition to the personnel roster. "Look at that Anton Crotch."

"I think his name is Tanton Skroch."

"Whatever. That guy gives new meaning to the word mooning."

They both studied Tanton for a moment. He was a couple of years older than the rest of the Roast Bean's young staff, built like a brick wall, with black hair slicked back from a pale and receding brow, and never let John Sunderland out of his sight for even a single second.

"Puppy love," said Emily with a smile. "So cute."

"Not so cute to me," spoke a voice behind them.

Both Clara and Emily looked up. They'd been joined by Teddy Lynett, the coffee shop's manager. Teddy was a weaselly little man with a distinct overbite and a spotty complexion. And if that wasn't bad enough, at thirty-four he was fast becoming bald.

"Don't you like it when young people are in love, Teddy?" asked Clara.

"Not when they're on my payroll I don't," Teddy said, darting annoyed glances at both Tanton and John. "I pay those morons to serve the customers, not to act out some hormonal fantasy." And with these words, he stalked over to John and Justyna, clearly with the intention of breaking up the budding lovefest.

"Teddy's right," said Clara. "We're here to work, not flirt."

Emily laughed. "You mean, Justyna is here to work, not flirt with your crush."

"I don't have a crush," said Clara. "I just think Justyna is very unprofessional, that's all." And with these words, she deftly picked up a tray she'd prepared, and sashayed away.

John and Justyna, their little tryst rudely interrupted by Teddy, moved in opposite directions. John joined Emily behind the counter, while Justyna took a customer's order.

"That Teddy is such a bore," said John with an eyeroll. "Doesn't he realize there are more important things in the world than work, work, work all the time?"

Emily studied her young colleague for a moment. With his strong jawline, clear blue eyes and perfectly coiffed dark hair with fashionable highlights, he could have been a male model. She didn't know a whole lot about him, except that he was studying at Columbia, and that he'd suddenly turned up at the Community Arts School out of the blue.

"You don't like Teddy?" Emily asked now.

John shrugged, picked up a brownie, and took a bite. "I do not like bullies."

John had a strong accent, possibly Eastern European. It was different from Ansel's, though, who was Ukrainian. "Teddy is not a bully," said Emily. "He's just trying to make this place work."

"I still say he is a bully," said John with an intent look at the manager. "Anyone who comes in the way of true love is a bully in my opinion."

From the corner of her eye, Emily saw that Tanton Skroch was still observing John intently. John, for his part, ignored the other man blithely. "Are you in love with Justyna?"

John arched a nicely shaped eyebrow. "Of course I'm in love. Isn't she the most gorgeous creature you've ever seen? That girl is an absolute grade-A stunner, is she not?"

"She is pretty," Emily conceded.

"Pretty?" John laughed. "That is an understatement, Emily Stone."

Emily was surprised John was aware of her surname. Then again, if there was any truth to his reputation as a ladies' man, he would pay attention to small details like that. "Where are you from, John?" she asked now.

He gave her an amused glance. "If I tell you I was American born and bred, you wouldn't believe me?"

"No, I wouldn't. Your accent... are you Russian?"

"Silvistanian. It is a small country located in the heart of the Caucasus." He turned to face her. "Now tell me about you, Emily Stone. Do you have a boyfriend? A lover? Husband perhaps?"

She laughed. "Not exactly."

"But you do have a roommate. Is he not your lover also?"

"Ansel? No way." She could have told John that Ansel played for the other team but that wasn't her story to tell.

John's attention didn't waver and she felt her cheeks redden under the scrutiny. "I don't understand. A beautiful young woman such as yourself. Why don't you have a boyfriend? Don't you like to love and be loved?" Then he snapped his fingers. "You and... Clara. You are girlfriends, yes? You are lovers?"

"No," she said with a frown. The last thing she wanted was to discuss her love life with a guy who'd just professed his undying love for one of her colleagues. "Let's just say I haven't found the right one yet."

John smiled a knowing smile. "Go out with me tonight, Emily Stone. I have lots and lots of friends. I'm very certain you will find the right one amongst them. They are all very handsome and very rich."

"I'm volunteering at the school tonight, remember? And you're modeling."

"Afterwards. We will paint this town blue and you will fall in love and be happy!"

"Paint the town red, you mean."

He did the jazz hands thing. "All the colors of the rainbow for you!"

She had to smile at his enthusiasm. "Won't Justyna be jealous if you ask me out?"

"Oh, but Justyna is coming, too."

"What about your admirer?" she said, indicating Tanton Skroch.

John made a throwaway gesture with his hand. "Oh, don't mind him."

Clara had joined them and Emily thought there were actual stars in her friend's eyes as she stood staring at John.

"Can I come, too?" Clara asked, a little piteously.

"Of course! The more the better," said John. He tapped Clara on the nose. "You will find love tonight, Clara Collett. We will all drink and be merry and live happily ever after."

"I would like that," said Clara, gushing.

"Oh, for crying out loud," said Teddy. "When are you people going to understand that you're here to work and not pretend you're the cast from Mamma Mia?"

John gave Emily a wink. "What did I tell you? Work, work, work!"

"Chop, chop, chop," said Teddy. "Or else you'll all live without a job ever after." He directed a scathing look at John. "And who's going to pay for your highlights then, sunshine?"

Chapter Two

That night, Emily saw a lot of familiar faces at the art school. John was there, of course, and so was Justyna, whom apparently he'd invited to join the class. Tanton Skroch was there, clearly as fixated on his male crush as he'd been at the coffee shop, and Emily even though she recognized a Roast Bean customer in a young and stern-faced young man with a hooknose and eyes so dark they almost appeared black.

Possibly another one of John Sunderland's many admirers, be they male or female.

The place where the life drawing class took place on a weekly basis was a large, airy and cozily cluttered room on the ground floor of the Community Arts School, tucked away near the back, with a view of a small inner-city garden, and the red-brick back walls of neighboring houses. Easels had been placed in a semi-circle around a dais where a table had been placed for the model to relax for the two hours that the class usually ran.

The walls were covered with artwork from current and previous students, some accurately depicting the human form, others... not so much. There were a few drawings of John's backside, according to some his most fetching feature, and a lot of other models. The school's janitor Adelric Lidd, a bushy-browed rail-thin septuagenarian, shuffled in and out of the room, helping Emily and Judyta Kenworthy, the art teacher, to organize the class.

Judyta was a striking woman of middle age, with remarkable green eyes, sharp-cut features, and invariably dressed in brightly colored kaftans. Today she was resplendent in turquoise, accessorizing her garb with a string of pearls and a burgundy headdress. Emily, dressed as usual in jeans and a shapeless but comfy sweater, felt positively underdressed.

"I thought we were going out?" asked John when he caught sight of her.

"I live just around the corner," she explained. "I'll just pop home and change."

"Of course you could always go out in that," he said, casting a critical eye at her orange Brooklyn College sweater. "I'm sure it's very... American."

And with these words, he turned away from her and joined Justyna, who was looking more like Barbie than ever, with her platinum hair and her immaculately made-up face.

"Are you and John going out tonight, dear?" asked old Sylvia Koss, who was the class's most loyal pupil. She'd been coming to class for many many years, and was one of its most gifted students, her artistic talent unrivaled after so much practice.

"Yeah. He wants to introduce me to some of his friends," said Emily, setting up the extra easels Adelric had just hoisted in. John's popularity had created a unique problem: not enough easels for all the new signups. So Adelric had raided one of the daytime art classes for extra easels and chairs.

"Oh, lucky you," said Sylvia with a twinkle in her eye. She was a kindly old lady with cotton candy white hair, a cheerful pink face and a perpetual smile.

Emily smiled. "I'm not so sure. If all of John's friends are like him, I'll have to beat them off with a stick."

"Yes, he is very affectionate, isn't he?"

"That's one word for it," she said as she watched John turn up the flirtatious energy full-tilt, Justyna simpering under the onslaught.

"I used to know a young man just like him," said Sylvia. "I used to be a shopkeeper's assistant, you know, before my retirement. We had temps coming in all the time—many eager to learn the trade, but also many just so they could be near the other, female temps." She nodded knowingly. "And of course girls just so they could catch the eye of the boys."

"It drives my manager crazy," said Emily.

"Oh, well, what can you do," said Sylvia philosophically. "Love turns us all into fools."

Just then, Judyta came waltzing up, her kaftan rustling.

"Please take your positions," she said, clapping her hands sharply. "We're about to begin. You, too, John, dear, please."

John seemed reluctant to part with his conquest, but he did as he was told, and moved towards the partition placed in a corner of the room where he could undress.

Sylvia brought out a small thermos of herbal tea and poured out a cup.

People had been chatting and moving about the room, most of the activity centered around the rickety plastic folding table that the janitor had set up near the door and that carried large push button thermoses filled with coffee and tea. Plates with cookies and even a chocolate cake accompanied them, all home-baked and provided by the attendants.

Usually by the time the class was over only dregs and crumbs remained. One of the reasons people loved Judyta's art classes was that she provided a fun, relaxed atmosphere. No pressure to be perfect. Even people without an ounce of talent were most welcome.

John emerged from behind the partition, not wearing a stitch, and Sylvia hurried towards him, carrying the cup of tea. He took it gratefully, gulped it down, and handed back the cup. It was a ritual Sylvia had perfected: a cup of herbal tea to relax the 'talent,' so they could last the long session on the podium.

All eyes had turned to John as he mounted the stage, hopped onto the table and stretched himself out, buttocks to the audience, front to the high windows, and adjusted his position until he was perfectly comfortable.

He then shot a quick look over his shoulder. "Ready when you are, Mrs. Kenworthy."

A collective sigh went through the room at the sight of all of this male perfection, and people were quick to take their position behind their easels.

"Best buns in the business," one of the attendants whispered to her neighbor.

"I heard that," said John with a grin. "And you're right, of course, Mrs. Franklin."

Mrs. Franklin, an elderly lady with four grandchildren, blushed appropriately.

"Shush, John," said Judyta Kenworthy sternly, adjusting her kaftan. "Class, begin."

John flexed his buttocks good-naturedly, drawing gasps from his captive audience, and then he relaxed into his pose, and only the scratching of pencil on paper was heard.

Emily joined Judyta in circling the class, giving encouragements here and little tips and tricks there, and generally allowing the students to settle into their own process of transferring the male form to the canvas in front of them. It took Emily only a glance to know that Tanton Skroch, for instance, was a lost cause. His frantic slashes had already resulted in three pencils being massacred, as well as a sheet of paper, and all he had to show for it was a stick figure that in no way, shape or form resembled John Sunderland.

The guy Emily had recognized as a regular customer of the Roast Bean was furiously stabbing at the paper with a passion that was probably better spent on a worthier cause. The end result was a Picassoesque monstrosity. Then Justyna was doing a much better job at it. Though she seemed entirely focused on John's buttocks, drawing them in increasingly widening circles and completely neglecting the rest of the young man's anatomy. Nor was she alone in this fixation. Other women, too, seemed fascinated by John's backside.

The only person who was creating something approximating realism was of course Sylvia, but then she'd seen so many male backsides the novelty had probably worn off.

"Very nice, Sylvia," whispered Emily, admiring the woman's lifelike drawing style.

"Thank you," said Sylvia, blushing happily. "I'm getting better at this, aren't I?"

Sylvia's modesty touched Emily. "I think you're aces," she said.

Sylvia gave her a confused look. "Aces is good, right?"

"Aces is excellent," she said, giving Sylvia two thumbs up.

Just at that moment, John coughed, and they all looked up. When he didn't stir, the work continued. People rose from their chairs for a refill of coffee or tea, or a slice of cake and a cookie, but apart from that, a companionable silence filled the room, accentuated by the soft classical music Judyta liked to play as background sound for her classes.

The two hours passed by quickly, and soon the time came to wrap things up.

Judyta clapped her hands again. "That's it, people. Great job. I'm proud of you."

All eyes went to the front of the class again, where John was now expected to descend from his throne, and put some more of that male goodness on display for his eager audience to see. Instead, John didn't move a muscle.

"John, dear," said Judyta, "you can come down now."

When John still didn't make any attempt to disengage, giggles went up.

"I think he's fallen asleep," said Mrs. Franklin.

"Better wake him up, Em," said Judyta.

Emily walked up to the stage, a smile on her lips. It wasn't the first time a model had dozed off in the middle of a session. Judyta always arranged for the thermostat to be turned up, so resident models didn't get goosebumps or, worse, pneumonia, and the warmth, combined with the murmur of activity and Sylvia's herbal concoction, had a soporific effect.

"John?" she said as she approached the stage. "You can get up now. Class is over." When he didn't respond, she mounted the dais and bent over him. "John? Did you fall asleep?"

And that's when she saw it: something was sticking out of his eye.

She frowned, at first not understanding what she was seeing.

When she did, her blood suddenly ran cold.

John wasn't sleeping. He was dead.

Chapter Three

The police arrived in short order. They took down the class participants' information and then herded them all into an adjacent classroom while they descended upon Judyta's room which was now, outrageously enough, deemed a crime scene.

"I can't believe this," Judyta said, pacing the room, her kaftan flapping about her heels. She was wearing sandals, Emily now saw. Not that it mattered. She'd gratefully accepted a cup of Sylvia's tea and was taking healing sips. According to the old lady it would soothe her nerves. She was, after all, the one who'd discovered John's body.

The moment she had, the others had all moved forward in tandem, and the cries of dismay and horrified shock had quickly rent the air, until Judyta had had the presence of mind to call the emergency services. Tanton Skroch had been most shocked of all. His eyes had practically popped out of his skull when he saw what had happened to the object of his affection. He'd uttered a blood-curdling scream that seemed quite out of character, and had immediately grabbed his phone and started spewing a stream of words in a strange language into the device, raking a distraught hand through his hair and looking very upset.

He wasn't looking much better now, seated on a chair, leaning forward, a distant look in his eyes, his mouth set, his right leg shaking. The man was obviously very rattled.

Justyna, too, appeared unnerved. She still looked like Barbie in the flesh, but she was pale and drawn now, and chewing her lip as she gazed out of the window into the dark night. The class participants had settled down in clusters of threes and fours, and were talking in hushed tones about the tragic events that had put an abrupt end to the evening.

"Who could have done this?" Judyta addressed the question at no one in particular.

"And how?" added Sylvia. She turned to Emily. "Did you see anyone going up to that poor young man?"

Emily shook her head. She'd been going over the evening in her mind, but at no point had she seen anyone approach the front of the class. She would have noticed if anyone had.

"It's a mystery," said Judyta. "An absolute mystery."

"They must have shot that bolt through the window," said Emily.

"But the windows are intact," said Sylvia. "Aren't they?"

Emily had to admit that they were. Judyta was right. It was baffling.

"The police will figure it out," she said. "They always do."

"Hah! I'm not so sure," said Judyta, who didn't seem to have a lot of confidence in the NYPD. "If we can't figure this out, neither can they."

"I'm sure they can," said Emily. "They have all that high-tech CSI stuff. I'm sure there's a perfectly reasonable explanation for what happened."

She felt horrible. And partially responsible. After all, she was Judyta's assistant. And now one of their models was dead. Murdered. Right in front of their eyes.

"This is all my fault," she said therefore.

"Now, now," said Sylvia, placing a soothing hand on her shoulder. "Don't say that."

"I should have noticed something was wrong."

"Of course not. How could you?" The old lady mused for a moment. "That young man must have had enemies. Why else would anyone go to all this trouble to murder him?"

"I don't think it has anything to do with him," said Judyta. "Some... *maniac* wanted to draw blood and so he did. Whether it was John or someone else didn't matter. Not in the least. I'll tell you what I think. I think this was the work of a serial killer. Perfecting the perfect kill. Serial killers are always doing this sort of thing. Showing off their murderous skill set. Proving their superiority. I'll bet the police know exactly who's behind this and why. They probably even have a nickname for him. The Crossbow Killer or something."

"You read entirely too many James Patterson novels, my dear," said Sylvia.

"Excuse me," Emily muttered, suddenly not feeling well, and quickly getting up. As she headed for the door, she heard Sylvia say, "Really, dear. Can't you see the poor girl's upset?"

The officer parked at the door looked up when she opened it. "I'm afraid you'll have to stay put, miss," he said.

"I need to use the bathroom," she said. "I don't feel so good."

He must have noticed she was about to pass out, for he barked, "Jackson! Take her to the bathroom, will you?"

Jackson, a jolly-faced youth, did as he was told, and escorted her to the bathroom, then took up position outside while she splashed some water on her face and then sank down on the toilet seat. She wasn't usually the squeamish type, but this murder business had really done a number on her. Her legs felt like jelly, and her stomach was tied up into knots.

As she sat quietly, her head in her hands, trying to regain

her composure, she heard distinct voices from the other side of the thin wall behind her.

"Nasty business," said a gruff male voice.

"Baffling, too," said another, equally gruff male voice.

"What about the wall?"

"Not a blemish. Windows, too. Not a scratch on them."

"That bolt must have come from somewhere, Shakespeare."

"I know, sir, but it can't have passed through brick or glass, can it?"

"No, I suppose you're right. What about a device built *into* the wall?"

"We went over that wall with a magnifying glass, sir."

"And?"

"Nothing."

"What about the table?"

"Perfectly ordinary table, sir. Besides, according to the trajectory that bolt *must* have come through the window. There's no other way. Must have."

There was a momentary silence, then: "Baffling. Just like you say, Shakespeare."

"Exactly, sir."

A toilet was flushed, and the voices died away.

Emily emerged from the stall and moved over to the sink. She splashed some more water on her face and pulled some paper napkins from the dispenser. She dabbed them at her face and looked up. Looking back at her wasn't the fresh-faced and shiny visage she knew. Instead, she was pale and puffy-eyed. Even her brown hair hung limp and lifeless. She shook her head. What a terrible business.

She joined the others again, and saw that Tanton Skroch was gone. Probably called in for his police interview. Sylvia was still chatting with Judyta, and she joined them. Sylvia had brought out her wallet and was showing pictures of her goddaughters, all tucked into a foldable picture holder. There were at least a dozen.

"And this is Ellie," she was saying. "She has kids of her own now."

Emily made an effort to smile. "I didn't know you had so many goddaughters."

"Oh, yes, I do," said the old lady proudly. She pointed at another picture. "This is Mollie. My friend Natalie's little girl. She was born on Christmas Eve."

"A Christmas baby," said Emily.

"What about that cat?" asked Judyta, tapping a picture of a cat which had apparently slipped into the collection.

"That's Gemini," said Sylvia with visible affection. "She's my precious baby."

She would have told them a lot more but at that moment the officer opened the door and bellowed, "Emily Stone. Miss Emily Stone!"

Emily shot up. "That's me."

"They're ready for you now," said the officer.

She glanced back at the others, who all sat looking at her anxiously. Then Sylvia gave her a pat. "You'll do just fine, dear."

"Tell them about my serial killer theory," said Judyta. "Or better yet, don't. I'll tell them myself." She nodded self-importantly. "Oh, I'll tell them!"

Emily walked out of the room and was directed into a spacious classroom, the door closed after her. Two police officers were impatiently waiting, seated behind the teacher's desk, a lone chair reserved for her. Judging from their scowls they weren't happy to see her.

ABOUT NIC

Nic Saint is the pen name for writing couple Nick and Nicole Saint. They've penned novels in the romance, cat sleuth, middle grade, suspense, comedy and cozy mystery genres. Nicole has a background in accounting and Nick in political science and before being struck by the writing bug the Saints worked odd jobs around the world (including massage therapist in Mexico, gardener in Italy, restaurant manager in India, and Berlitz teacher in Belgium).

When they're not writing they enjoy Christmas-themed Hallmark movies (whether it's Christmas or not), all manner of pastry, comic books, a daily dose of yoga (to limber up those limbs), and spoiling their big red tomcat Tommy.

www.nicsaint.com

Box Set 4 (Books 10-12)

Box Set 5 (Books 13-15)

Box Set 6 (Books 16-18)

Purrfect Santa

Purrfectly Flealess

Nora Steel

Murder Retreat

The Kellys

Murder Motel

Death in Suburbia

Emily Stone

Murder at the Art Class

Washington & Jefferson

First Shot

Alice Whitehouse

Spooky Times

Spooky Trills

Spooky End

Spooky Spells

Ghosts of London

Between a Ghost and a Spooky Place

Public Ghost Number One

Ghost Save the Queen

Box Set 1 (Books 1-3)

A Tale of Two Harrys

Ghost of Girlband Past

Ghostlier Things

Charleneland

Deadly Ride

Final Ride

Neighborhood Witch Committee

Witchy Start

Witchy Worries

Witchy Wishes

Saffron Diffley

Crime and Retribution

Vice and Verdict

Felonies and Penalties (Saffron Diffley Short 1)

The B-Team

Once Upon a Spy

Tate-à-Tate

Enemy of the Tates

Ghosts vs. Spies

The Ghost Who Came in from the Cold

Witchy Fingers

Witchy Trouble

Witchy Hexations

Witchy Possessions

Witchy Riches

Box Set 1 (Books 1-4)

The Mysteries of Bell & Whitehouse

One Spoonful of Trouble

Two Scoops of Murder

Three Shots of Disaster

Box Set 1 (Books 1-3)

A Twist of Wraith

A Touch of Ghost

A Clash of Spooks

Box Set 2 (Books 4-6)

The Stuffing of Nightmares

A Breath of Dead Air

An Act of Hodd

Box Set 3 (Books 7-9)

A Game of Dons

Standalone Novels

When in Bruges

The Whiskered Spy

ThrillFix

Homejacking

The Eighth Billionaire

The Wrong Woman